LATER,
AT THE BAR

A Novel in Stories

R E B E C C A   B A R R Y

SIMON & SCHUSTER
New York   London   Toronto   Sydney

SIMON & SCHUSTER
Rockefeller Center
1230 Avenue of the Americas
New York, NY 10020

SIMON & SCHUSTER and colophon are registered
trademarks of Simon & Schuster, Inc.

Designed by Carla Jayne Little

Manufactured in the United States of America

10 9 8 7 6 5 4 3 2 1

Library of Congress Cataloging-in-Publication Data

Barry, Rebecca, 1968–
    Later, at the bar : a novel in stories / Rebecca Barry.
        p.cm.
    ISBN-13: 978-1-4165-3524-9
    ISBN-10:   1-4165-3524-1
        1. Bars (Drinking establishments)—Fiction. 2. New York
        (State)—Fiction. I. Title.
    PS3602.A77758L38 2007
    813'.6—dc22

                                        2006051275

For information regarding special discounts for bulk
purchases, please contact Simon & Schuster Special Sales
at 1-800-456-6798 or business@simonandschuster.com

ACKNOWLEDGMENTS

I'd like to thank my mother for teaching me to love people's wildness, and my father for showing me how to look at the natural world with my heart. I am indebted to my husband, Tommy Dunne, for everything.

Many friends and colleagues, Dave Breeden, Hannah Tinti, Jeff Butler, Betsy Wheeler, and Sommer Sterud to name a few, provided inspiration, good ears, and perfect advice for these stories. I'd like to thank Terri Iacuzzo for seeing this book way before I did, and Erica Beeney for pushing it through its awkward adolescence with grace and a sharp eye.

I owe many thanks to Liz Gilbert, for making me want to write the book in the first place and then for reading ten thousand drafts and still being my friend, and to Barbara Jones for her continued support and for gently reminding me that I should be working on my book instead of writing her long e-mails.

My agent, Jin Auh, extended great patience, kindness, and good taste throughout this whole process and I am grateful to her, as well as my editor, Amanda Murray, who is a genius and also pretty fun.

I sincerely thank the faculty and students at the Ohio State University for providing support, wisdom, and excellent company, Erin McGraw and Lee Martin in particular. And of course, none of this would have happened if Lee K. Abbott, whose fingerprints are all over this collection, hadn't sat me down on a hot summer day and said, "Write this book. Now."

CONTENTS

Lucy's Last Hurrah   1

Men Shoot Things to Kill Them   9

Snow Fever   43

Newspaper Clipping   67

Love Him, Petaluma   73

Grace   101

Not Much Is New Here   123

How to Save a Wounded Bird   161

Instructions for a Substitute Bus Driver   183

Eye. Arm. Leg. Heart.   195

LATER,
AT THE BAR

LUCY'S LAST HURRAH

That winter there were two snowstorms. The first one was expected. Born in Florida and galvanized by the damp winds of the Pennsylvania mountains, it was strong as a wildcat by the time it reached upstate New York. The YMCA closed early and so did the library. The mayor declared a state of emergency, which it was. There were three head-on collisions on Route 19 and a teenager froze to death after falling into one of the gorges on the north end of town. Hank Stevens, who owned Hank's Diner, couldn't get out of his driveway and had to stay at home with his children. ("No," he said all afternoon. "Daddy cannot go outside and build a fort. Daddy doesn't own snow pants.")

Hank called Bill Kane, who made the soups and

burgers at the diner, and told him to stay home. Bill had already assumed Hank would close the diner early because as far as he was concerned his boss was a lazy man who looked for excuses to lose money. But he went to the diner anyway, because it was nicer than his own apartment, and called his ex-girlfriend Trish to see if she needed help shoveling or with anything, really. But when a man answered the phone, Bill hung up and went next door to Lucy's Tavern—which was never closed because Rita, the bartender, lived upstairs—and got blind drunk instead.

The second storm blew in from nowhere a few weeks later, and no one, not even the weather girl on Channel 7, saw it coming. The day started out clear, but by noon the air was heavy and raw, and by four o'clock the sky had turned steel gray. By five, as Hank Stevens, Bill Kane, and the other regulars filed into Lucy's Tavern for happy hour, the snow began to fall.

At seven-thirty, Lucy Beech, the founder of Lucy's Tavern, was awakened from the dream state she'd been in and out of for several days. She heard the windows rattling and saw the snowflakes whirling like madmen. She listened to the wind howling and it sounded familiar, like the melancholy cries of the wolves that used to greet her on the one hundred acres of woodland where she grew up in Alaska. That sound always made her feel at home, and now it seemed as if it was beckoning her, saying *get up, come outside, come see this miraculous storm.*

Lucy was eighty-two and her bones were tired, but she got out of bed and walked outside wearing only her nightgown and no shoes. Snow hit her face. Cold hurt her teeth. The fierce, bitter wind reminded her of the storms of her youth, and she sat down on a snowbank and waited.

Lucy's obituary appeared several days later next to the police monitor, which reported three DWIs, one burglary, and an arrest of a woman whose cat was "defecating in an annoying manner" on her neighbor's front porch. The obituary was short, as Lucy would have liked it, but it was written by her cousin who lived in Topeka and didn't know her very well. It hardly mentioned the tavern Lucy established, or how—because Lucy loved live music and dancing and understood people who liked longing more than they did love—it became the center of the community.

It didn't talk about Lucy's late partner Suzanne, who died a month before Lucy and was buried in the garden by a slender birch. (Like many women in that town, and perhaps the world over, Lucy fell in love with a handsome woman after years of loving men.) Instead it mentioned Lucy's fine hand at embroidery, her moral upbringing, and her decent sense of community service.

In its own way, the bar Lucy built did service the community. The place itself was nothing special—a narrow room on the first floor of a brick building that had once been an apothecary. It had hardwood floors and mullioned windows, and when Lucy bought it, the floor-to-ceiling apothecary shelves and cabinets were still there, flanking a long beveled mirror and facing a wooden counter, which Lucy decided would make a good bar. She was in her twenties then, an Alaskan fisherwoman with proud cheekbones and long dark hair that she wore in two shiny braids. Rumor had it that she had been so skilled at fishing that she'd once taught an orphaned bear cub to hunt salmon. But she'd given that up to come east with her boyfriend, a noisy, failed actor who wanted to start a dance hall. They bought the storefront next to Hank's Diner, and because it was mostly Lucy who paid for it they called it Lucy's.

Some people said the bar was cursed because Lucy's boyfriend left town with a milliner six months later, leaving Lucy heartbroken and alone, miles away from the Northern lights and the midnight sun and all the things she used to love. But Lucy, who stayed in upstate New York—a place known for its brutal winters and triumphant springs—laughed at this. After all, even salmon swam upstream to spawn. Heartache, to her, coursed through everything— which was as it should be, since people needed it to make them kind.

Over the years Lucy built her bar into an open front parlor full of music and drinking, where bad behavior within reason was perfectly acceptable. She knew how to use both the gun and the baseball bat she kept under the bar by the cash register and she didn't judge her patrons as long as they paid their bills. Although once or twice she may have offered her opinion. "You know, Martin, most of us learn in grade school that saying things like 'I'm so *lonely*' doesn't impress women," she might have said. And when Hank Stevens sat at the bar saying things about his wife like "You wouldn't complain about the smoke at a strip club the way *she* does," she might have responded with, "I would if I was seven months pregnant." To her, the bar was like a good wedding, where love, sex, hope, and grief were just in the air and everyone who breathed it in was drunk not just on booze but the smoky haze around them.

So, cursed or not, Lucy's Tavern was the place most people in town came to lick their wounds or someone else's, or to give in to the night and see what would happen. Lucy grew older and her body thickened. Her once nimble feet grew arthritic and gnarled as the roots of the poplars that lined the streets in the center of town. But her skin, which rarely saw the light of day, stayed youthful and high colored even as her dark braids turned gray, then white. The bar aged too—the hardwood floors became seasoned and polished from dancing and fighting. The mirror grew mottled and reflected a softer, more flattering image of the people it faced. Eventually a gallery of stuffed birds—a crow, a turkey, a proud kingfisher—that Lucy's partner Suzanne, an ornithologist, had collected appeared at the top of the bar.

By the time that second snowstorm hit, Lucy had long since turned the bar over to her bartender, Rita. So none of her regulars knew she was quietly freezing to death that night, as they drifted in for happy hour and stayed out until dawn, taking shelter from the snow and the wind that shook the buildings.

Later, when they were at the bar toasting Lucy's life, the regulars said she was in that wind, mingling with the smell of wood smoke and pine. They said she swept over the graveyards and apple orchards, on to Main Street, past the old brick row houses. They said they felt her make her way by Hank's Diner, then by her bar, where she rode in on the icy air that came off of people's jackets and lingered in the clouds of smoke and perfume. She might have been struck, as she often had been when she was running the place herself, by the rough and beautiful ways people carried their loneliness. She might have breathed into the air, touched a cheek. *It's all right,* she might have said. *The heart is right to cry. Oh, darlings, enjoy the night.* She might have considered staying, at least until daybreak, but the wind picked up again and pulled her back into the storm.

The morning after the storm, the sun came out and the sky turned a brilliant blue.

"No," Hank Stevens said to his children. "Daddy does not want to go outside. Daddy is going to make a ham sandwich, and then he is going to lie down."

"This fucking town," Bill Kane said, looking at his

snow-covered driveway. "No wonder people kill themselves here every winter."

It was Harlin Wilder, delivering Meals on Wheels as part of his community service, who found Lucy in her front yard in her nightgown, stiff and blue and dead, her face tilted upward, her hands tucked neatly beneath her thighs, as if she were waiting for something wonderful to happen.

Men Shoot Things to Kill Them

Three months after his divorce from his first wife became final, Harlin Wilder's new wife Grace left town with another man. Her reasons were solid enough. She was going to bowl in a tournament in Chemung County, and Jimmy Slocum, who was heading up there with a truckload of salt, had offered her a ride.

"It's free," said Grace, who had wrecked her own car a few weeks before. "How often do you get to say you're getting a free ride and mean it?"

Harlin didn't answer. He didn't like Jimmy's flinty eyes or oily curls, or the way he rolled up his shirtsleeves to show off his biceps. And Harlin was pretty sure this wasn't a free ride. In fact, he figured that it would cost about $59.99 plus tax, or whatever they were charging at the Econo Lodge out that way. But he kept his mouth shut, as it was his jealousy that had gotten him in trouble with his last wife, who had cleaned out his bank account and run off with a car salesman. Harlin had tried not to hold this against her, because Sherry was a good-looking woman, and good-looking women got a lot of offers. He'd figured the best he could do was stay out of trouble and wait for her to come home.

And that's what he had been doing, waiting for his ex-wife, when he met Grace, who drove a food truck for the state prison. It had been a long, dull winter, but that night there was a snap in the air that hadn't been around since fall. The jukebox was turned up and people were already dancing by happy hour. Cyrus Wilder, Harlin's older brother by fifteen minutes, was buying rounds, an event so rare that Harlin kept asking other regulars to sign a napkin witnessing the occasion. Even this didn't rile Cyrus, who had shaved his winter beard and slicked his gray hair back off his forehead. He'd won three hundred dollars at a dogfight and was feeling like a benevolent king.

Harlin was sitting there, pleasantly drunk and enjoying his brother's good mood, when he heard the song "All My Exes Live in Texas" on the jukebox. It occurred to him that two of his exes did live in Texas, and this made him feel a warm kinship to the person who played that song.

"Rita," he said to the bartender, "I would like to buy whoever played this song a shot."

Rita put down the glass she was drying and said, "Did you hear that, Grace? This man wants to buy you a drink."

Grace glanced up from a conversation just long enough for a quick appraisal of Harlin. "I'm done drinking for the night," she said.

Harlin Wilder was a tall man, and well-proportioned, with muscled arms, a trim waist, and quick, strong legs. His dark hair was flecked with gray, prematurely, like that of his father and brother, and he had a tidy mustache he wore to hide a slight harelip. He had a wide and engaging smile, which, after years of getting him into bed with women and out of evictions and jail sentences, was starting to etch graceful lines around his eyes and the sides of his mouth. If Grace hadn't looked at him, Harlin might not have cared what she said, but the fact that she looked him over and then refused made him take more stock in her. She was nice to look at, he decided. Not nice to look at in the way the bartender, Rita, with her auburn curls and easy laugh, was, and not nice to look at the way Linda Hartley, who wouldn't set foot in the bar without high heels and a soft sweater, was. Grace Meyers was nice to look at in an unreachable way. Her face was long and pretty, in spite of a pointed chin, and a dangerous heat came off of her, murky and wild, like a swamp. She had nice tits, too, and while Harlin didn't like to think he was picky, he did appreciate a big set of those.

He tried to buy her a drink a few more times over the next few weeks, but she refused. Then one night she gave in, and they ended up in her food truck, having sex on a pile of dirty aprons. Grace left her boyfriend and started seeing Harlin, and they'd gone on a bender one weekend and that's how they ended up married. And now she was going off to another city with another man.

"I don't care if he is her good friend and they *are* going to a bowling tournament," Harlin said later that night to Linda Hartley. They were sitting at Lucy's Tavern, eating goldfish crackers. "Why would a woman want to go to another city with another man and spend the night there? You tell me."

"Have you tried talking to her?" Linda asked. Linda was an advice columnist and advocated communication. She took off her glasses and smoothed her hair, which she wore parted on the side and up in the back like a librarian. A naughty librarian, Harlin imagined. Or hoped.

He shrugged. Some people at the bar, he knew, weren't too crazy about Linda Hartley. Harlin's brother Cyrus, for example, thought she asked too many questions and didn't drink enough. Hank Stevens agreed. He said that that was the trouble with writers. They could never really let themselves go. But Harlin didn't mind her. She wore skirts and sweaters that showed off muscular legs and a shapely figure for a lady over thirty, and Harlin appreciated a woman who dressed up for the bar.

Harlin's brother Cyrus suggested that they get into Harlin's truck and drive up to Lodi to shoot out Jimmy's tires.

"We can do a tour of the bars along the way," Cyrus said, listing a little to one side. He adjusted the black knit fisherman's cap that fit snugly over his head. Cyrus was Harlin's fraternal twin. He was shorter than Harlin, but stronger and more classically handsome. At forty-three his face had begun to age. But his eyes, heavy-lidded and smoky blue, still made him look dreamy. "All of the old places," he said.

"That's a stupid idea," said Linda. "Why drive all the way to Lodi to do something you could just as easily do here?"

"Who asked you?" Cyrus said.

"Harlin did," she said calmly.

"Not really," Harlin said.

"Anyway," Linda said, "if you drive out there and shoot out his tires, she'll have an excuse to spend the night there."

Harlin looked at Cyrus for another suggestion, but Cyrus was watching his ex-wife Janet, who was sitting at the bar talking about the president.

"If I was the president and I got caught with my dick in someone's mouth, I would lie about it," she was saying.

"Janet, you don't lie," said the woman next to her.

"I know I don't lie," said Janet. "But if I was the president I would have to, which is why I am not the president and I am sitting here at this bar with this bunch of losers." She looked pointedly at Cyrus, who waved.

There were several other suggestions: Go to Jimmy Slocum's house to see if Grace and Jimmy were already back, try to pick up another girl in town, or drink a cup of coffee and go home and lie down. This last suggestion came from Rita, the bartender, who was getting ready to close and was sick of listening to all of them. None of these seemed satisfactory to Harlin, but he did listen to Rita, since she followed her advice with "And if you don't, I'm using my bat."

The next afternoon, when Harlin was having breakfast, Cyrus showed up with a gun, two bottles of Wild Turkey, and a bowling ball he'd gotten at his first bachelor party, when his friends attached it to his leg with a chain and made him walk around town trying to pick up women.

"Get in, Harlin," he said. "We're going to see your old lady bowl."

Harlin thought briefly of Cyrus's lawyer and what he might say if Cyrus got busted driving drunk again six months after a DWI.

"I don't know if this is a good idea," Harlin said.

"When was the last time either of us had a good

idea?" Cyrus said. And Harlin high-fived him and got into the car.

They pulled out of the driveway and onto the road, and as they passed the Grange Hall, Harlin started thinking out loud. The trouble with his new wife, he said, was that she had terrible taste in men. Just look at the last three men she'd been with before him. First there was Sonny Banfield, who had a nasty temper and loved cockfighting; then Marty Chambers, who owed everyone money; and then she married Nick Fowler, *Fowler*, who everyone knew treated women like dirt. And now she was running around with Jimmy Slocum, with his dumb, thick hands and greasy smile.

"Slocum!" Cyrus said, taking a drink from the bottle of Wild Turkey. "I hate that guy."

"He has mean dogs," Harlin said. "You can't trust a man with mean dogs."

It wasn't Grace's fault, Harlin went on. Her father was a violent man, and her mother hadn't stopped him from beating his children, and that was why Grace had dated two men who hit her and one who stole her money.

"You sure she's cheating on you?" Cyrus said.

"No, I'm not sure," Harlin said, annoyed. "If I was sure, I'd shoot Jimmy, not his tires."

Cyrus nodded. They passed the old high school, which was being renovated because the county was getting richer. This part of the world was changing, Harlin thought. When he and Cyrus were young, it had been full of cornfields and livestock and fantastic drunks like Harlin's dad, who jumped through plate-glass windows and set fire to abandoned houses. Now the landscape was being eaten up by new houses big enough for three families, with treeless front lawns and oversize plastic play sets.

Cyrus turned left onto the dead-end road that went past Janet's house.

"Oh, Jesus," Harlin said. "Cyrus. Don't be stupid."

"I just want to stop by and say hello," Cyrus said.

"You broke up with Nancy four days ago," Harlin said. "Don't you think it's a little early to go visit your ex-wife?"

"Who died and made you my mother?" Cyrus said.

"Mom." It had been long enough since their mother had died that they could both laugh, but then they were quiet until Cyrus pulled into the driveway of an old farmhouse. The windows in the front of the house were open, and someone inside was playing Hank Williams.

"Hey, you little margarita!" Cyrus yelled. "Hey, you

sweet potato pie!" Someone inside turned the music up. "Hey, you hot, spicy bowl of chili!"

Janet opened the door and squinted at them. She was tall and stooped, with a narrow, fine-boned face and ruddy cheeks passed on from her Irish father. "What the fuck do you want?" she said.

"Hi, Janet," Harlin said.

"What's new, Harlin?" she said. She blew her nose into a Kleenex.

"You look like a ray of sunshine!" Cyrus said.

Janet put the Kleenex in her pocket.

"We're going on a road trip," Cyrus said. "A fantastic ride. We're going to hit five bars in this county, and then we're going to Lodi to check out a bowling tournament."

"You can't bowl," said Janet.

"That's why we thought of you," Cyrus said.

Janet had been a champion bowler. At Lucy's Tavern, which had inherited all of the pictures from the bowling alley after it closed down, there were photos of Janet along the exposed brick wall between the piano and the jukebox. She was maybe twenty-two years old, her bobbed hair neatly tucked behind her ears, her long body gracefully curved to make the ball hit its target. Once Harlin had seen

Cyrus point out those pictures to a stranger at the bar.

"That's my ex-wife," he'd said. "I married her twice and she divorced me twice. How do you like that? A champion ball handler and I let her go." He'd shaken his head, and the stranger had looked uncomfortable. Finally, Rita had told him he needed to shut up or she was taking the picture down.

Janet stalked back into the house, and since she hadn't told them to leave, Harlin and Cyrus followed her. Her kitchen was painted green, and newspapers littered the table.

"What do you say, Jan?" Cyrus said. "Why don't you come with us?"

"Why should I go anywhere with you?" Janet said.

"For fun," Cyrus said. "When was the last time you just let yourself have a lost day?"

Janet put her cigarette out and turned to face Cyrus. Her pale eyes, gray-blue like winter, narrowed.

"We used to do that sometimes," he said. "Remember?"

Cyrus was handsome then, and Harlin remembered how beautiful his brother had been in his prime. He'd had strong arms and thick black hair and was the kind of good-looking that made farming seem like the only real work for a man's body. But then he drank too much and fought too much, and now his face was beginning to look like it had hit the pavement too many times. Sometimes, though, like here in Janet's green kitchen, Harlin saw a glimpse of what his brother had been and it made his throat ache.

Janet sighed. "All right," she said. "Only if you promise I'll be back by ten."

"You got it," Cyrus said. "Or midnight."

They got into the car and drove on, and Janet put some Johnny Cash on the tape deck. She and Cyrus sang, and Harlin kept time on the back of Cyrus's headrest.

"Rita wanted to close the bar to come with us," Cyrus said. "That's how great this trip will be."

"Goddammit, Cyrus," Janet said. "What did you give her ammunition for? I can just see the jaws down there flapping. 'Oh, Janet starts drinking at three.' Well, some days I start drinking at ten. Sometimes I start at six-thirty a.m. She doesn't need to know that."

"Janet," Cyrus said softly. "You don't start at six-thirty."

"Maybe some days I do," Janet said.

They drove by a bar called the Stove Pipe, and Janet said she was thirsty. Harlin thought maybe they should save the Stove Pipe for the way back, after they'd picked up Grace. But Janet insisted, and since Grace had once called the Stove Pipe a shit bucket, Harlin decided it was all right if they went to this one place without her.

The Stove Pipe had been a chicken coop before it was a bar and had such a low ceiling that people wrote graffiti on it instead of on the bathroom walls. *What in the hell are you looking up here for? Lisa is a slut.—Well, stop the presses.* There was only one other customer in the room, a man named Moneybags because he was always hitting people up for cash, who Harlin used to work with when he was a hired man on a horse farm. Moneybags was one of those guys whose skin had darkened from the work he did, but it had always been hard for Harlin to tell whether he was tan or just constantly covered in a fine layer of dirt. He had prominent front teeth and light green eyes, and he drove his tractor everywhere.

They said hello to Moneybags, and Cyrus paid for Janet's beer.

"Now that's rare," said Janet and told Moneybags he might want to go see if his horses had sprouted wings. Moneybags laughed especially hard, since usually people made jokes like that at his expense. Then he asked them what they were doing over this way, and Harlin told him they were going to see his wife in a bowling tournament and maybe shoot out Jimmy Slocum's tires. Moneybags nodded slowly, like that seemed like a good idea.

"So you ended up marrying Grace?" he said. "Man. Everyone wants a piece of that lady."

Harlin didn't like the way he said that, as if he was just waiting for Harlin to die so he could get his hands on his new wife. He also figured Moneybags would have said "ass" instead of "lady" if Janet hadn't been there, and he didn't like that either.

"Watch your mouth, Moneybags," he said. "You're talking about my wife."

Moneybags raised his eyebrows and then his beer. "Nice work," he said. "She's a hard one to settle down." Harlin's back tightened.

"She cheats on everyone," Moneybags went on. "I mean Jimmy's a fool, don't get me wrong. But you can't blame him for trying."

"You trying to start something?" Harlin said. He remembered a lost chance to shove Moneybags in a pile of horseshit and regretted it.

"I ain't starting anything," Moneybags said. "I'm just saying that's a fine lady, that's all. Hard to hold on to."

"That's starting something in my book," Harlin said.

"Cool it, Harlin," Cyrus said. He signaled to the barmaid, who was on the phone, for another round. She gave him an openly hostile look and put the phone down.

"What's your name, cutie?" Cyrus said.

"Mitsy," she said. "Five dollars." She put the drinks down on the bar and waited for the money.

"Mitsy," Cyrus said, putting some bills on the bar. "Mitsy . . . Mitsy . . . didn't you do me once at a Motel Six?"

The bartender glanced at the clock, took the money, and went back to the phone.

"That's a great line, Cyrus," said Janet. "I bet that works all the time."

"I'm just kidding," Cyrus said. "She knows I'm kidding. Don't you, Mitsy?" Mitsy gave him the finger.

"Hey, Money, how's your boy?" said Cyrus.

"Weird," said Moneybags. "The kid can't stay focused. His mother thinks he has ADD, but I think either he's just an idiot or she should just unplug the goddamn television."

Harlin was about to say something about how the apple doesn't fall far from the tree so the kid was probably an idiot, but Janet cut him off.

"At least he's not like Hank Stevens's girl," she said, referring to the owner of the diner next to Lucy's. "They had to get rid of the dog because she kept sticking her fingers in its eyes. Then they got her a rabbit, and the other day he was on the phone at the bar saying, 'No, honey, don't put the bunny's head under water.'"

"That kid doesn't need a pet, she needs a cactus," said Moneybags.

Even Harlin had to laugh at that. He wasn't proud of it, but he liked it when other people had bad kids. He hadn't seen his own girl in years, didn't know what he'd say to her if he did, and other people's rotten kids made him proud of the child he didn't know.

Janet took some money from Cyrus's wallet and went over to the jukebox. Cyrus watched her go. Her wide, flat backside waved back at him like a parade.

"At least your kid isn't in a home like mine is," Cyrus said.

"Cyrus," Harlin said.

"What?" Cyrus said. "Everyone knows it. He couldn't take care of himself and we couldn't take care of him, and now he lives in a home with a bunch of retards."

Moneybags looked at his beer.

"No big deal," said Cyrus. "Right, Harlin?"

"Right," Harlin said, eyeing his brother carefully. Janet and Cyrus's boy, Colt, had been born with so many breathing problems that he'd lived in a crib on a respirator until he was fourteen. He spoke using raspy, unformed sounds, and he had stopped breathing and been declared dead and then resuscitated three different times before they finally put him in a home. It had caused the end of Cyrus's first marriage to Janet, and Harlin guessed the blame that coursed between them had something to do with the end of their second marriage, too.

Cyrus shrugged. "Just making conversation," he said.

Janet had put on some Jimmie Rodgers and swayed by the jukebox.

"That Janet," Cyrus said. "She has a mouth on her." He slurred a little, and Harlin could tell he was getting drunk. They were all headed that way, and it was only four o'clock.

"Ain't you been married to that woman twice?" said Moneybags.

"Yup," said Cyrus. "Look at her."

Janet wore a shapeless denim dress, and her hair hung lazily down her back. "She's sexy," said Cyrus.

"He broke up with his girlfriend four days ago," Harlin said.

"*She* broke up with *me*," Cyrus said.

Moneybags smiled at Harlin. "Talk about kicking a rock," he said.

Back in the car, Janet said, "Lord, the teeth on that Money. Were his parents woodchucks?"

It sounded like something Grace would say, which made Harlin like Janet. He sat back and looked out the window. They passed old, tired-looking houses with peeling paint, and farmers worrying about their livestock. Some people said this part of the state was depressing, but Harlin liked the fading majesty of the old farmhouses, and the way just past Chemung County the landscape broke free and stretched out for miles of rolling hills and wild creeks. Once he'd asked Grace why she moved back there from North Carolina, and she didn't answer right away. He'd wondered if she didn't know or wished she'd stayed down south. Finally she said, "I love the land." She lifted her shoulders helplessly. "That's what it is. It moves me, this part of the world." Harlin had made fun of her when she said that, and she had laughed at herself, but he knew what she meant and liked her for saying it the way she did.

In the front seat, Cyrus started haranguing his ex-wife. "Who are you dating these days, Jan? You still with that violin player?"

"Fiddler," said Janet.

"He's not a bad man," Cyrus said.

"He's a good man," Janet said.

They passed a farm, and Cyrus tooted the horn. "See that cow? I've driven by this farm six times in the last week and she ain't moved. She's got a hurt foot and they won't do anything about it."

"You need a job," Janet said.

"What's that guy's name again?" said Cyrus. "Dude? Dick?"

"Dan," Janet said.

"Staying out late, dancing with other women, is he?"

Janet reached into her pocket and pulled out a piece of gum.

"If I had you, I would never treat you that way," Cyrus said.

"You did treat me that way."

Harlin laughed. "She has a point," he said.

"Well, I wouldn't treat you like that anymore," said Cyrus.

"At least he doesn't end up in jail when he stays out late," Janet said.

"You still have a nice rack," Cyrus said. "You know that, Janet? A very nice set of potatoes."

"Keep your eyes on the road, Cyrus."

"No sir, I would not treat you that way ever again," Cyrus said. And as if to make his point, he took a swig from the bottle of Wild Turkey and graciously handed it to Janet.

They got to the bowling alley sometime around five and didn't see Jimmy's truck in the parking lot, which Janet noticed.

"I don't see Jimmy's truck," she said.

"That doesn't mean anything," Harlin said.

"It could mean you're paranoid," Janet said.

The bowling alley was an old one, and when they walked in, Janet got nostalgic. "I used to bowl here," she said to Cyrus. "Remember? I won a trophy here once. It was right after the second time Colty died."

"Sure I remember," Cyrus said, looking past Janet.

"Hotel California" was playing over the loud-speaker, and there was fake smoke coming from somewhere. Janet and Cyrus went over to the bowling lanes, and Harlin went to the bar, got himself a beer, and looked for Grace. Eventually he saw her near the coatrack, talking to her friend Bridget, a small woman with thick yellow hair and a catlike face. Grace was laughing, and Harlin got the familiar rush of panic and desire he always got when he saw her from a distance.

He walked toward her, his face settling into its wide, handsome grin. Grace walked over to meet him and put her hands around his waist. "Harlin," she said. "I didn't expect to see you here."

"Came to see you bowl," Harlin said.

"We finished an hour ago," Bridget said, peering out at him from underneath thick bangs.

"Did you win?" Harlin said.

"No," Grace said. "They cheated."

Out of the corner of his eye, Harlin could see that Janet had bought herself a game. She was standing with a ball, ready to roll it. Cyrus was looking at her ass.

"I'll go get my coat," Bridget said. "I'll wait for you outside."

Harlin stood in front of his wife, smiling at her like a fool. "You want a ride home?" he said.

"Sure," she said. "Where did you get a car?"

"Cyrus's driving."

Grace looked at Cyrus, who was whooping because Janet had gotten a strike. Janet told him to shut the hell up, it wasn't like she'd discovered a cure for cancer.

"Cyrus's drunk," she said.

"I guess I'll drive then," Harlin said.

"You're drunk," Grace said. She said it as if it wasn't the worst thing in the world, but Harlin took it the wrong way.

"What, did Slocum make you a better offer?"

A muscle in Grace's jaw tightened, the same one that tensed when her father called asking for money.

"What's that supposed to mean?" she said.

"Whatever you want it to mean," he said.

"Is that why you came up here?" Grace said. "To make sure I wasn't messing around with Jimmy?"

"I told you why I came up here," Harlin said. "I came here to see you bowl."

"Yeah, and you missed it," she said. "You missed it by an hour, because you stopped someplace to get loaded so you could come here and pick a fight."

"Cyrus was driving," Harlin said.

Grace picked up her bowling bag. "Right," she said. "That's your trouble, Harlin. It's always someone else's fault."

Harlin didn't really think a woman who cheated on every man she had ever been with should be telling someone who cared enough to marry her what his trouble was.

"A lot of women would be happy if their husband drove forty-five minutes to a different county to see them bowl," he said. "A lot of women would be happy if their husband cared about them enough to pick a fight with another man."

Grace gathered up her bag and her bowling shoes.

"I'm not a lot of other women," she said. "You should know that by now." She fished in her purse for a cigarette. "Bridget can drive me," she said. "I'll see you at home." And she left.

Harlin went over to sit with Janet and Cyrus. "How did it go with Grace?" Cyrus said.

"She has a ride home."

"Oh, Harlin," Janet said. She was holding a bowling ball, and the weight of it made her arm look long, like a chimp's. "You came all this way for nothing." She pulled back her arm and let the ball go. It wobbled down the lane and managed to miss the three pins that were still standing. Janet shook her head sadly. "That's it," she said. "I'm all washed up."

They got into the car, and Cyrus took the wheel. As they pulled out of town onto the main road, Cyrus and Janet began bickering again. "Seriously, Janet," Cyrus said. "What does Dave have that I don't?"

"A big penis," Janet said. "A job." She turned away from him to face Harlin.

"So what makes you think Grace is cheating on you?"

"I just don't think it's right for a woman to go to another county with a man who isn't her husband."

"Can't you trust her?" Janet said.

"Trust is important," Cyrus said.

Janet looked back at Cyrus. "Right. A wife should be able to trust her husband."

"What's that supposed to mean?" Cyrus said.

"Just what I said," said Janet.

Harlin opened his window a crack and breathed in the air. Summer was just giving way to fall and the air smelled like apples and goldenrod.

Cyrus stomped on the brakes, and Harlin almost broke his jaw on the back of Janet's seat. Harlin was about to tell his brother to learn how to drive when he heard Janet say, "Oh. Oh no. Oh, I can't bear it."

Harlin looked out the window and saw two Canada geese floundering in the middle of the road. Cyrus let out a whistle.

"They must have been flying low and gotten hit by a truck," he said.

Janet got out of the car. Harlin followed. They moved closer to the geese, and the male hissed, exposing a black tongue. Both geese were bleeding. The female was barely alive, her belly torn open. She made no sound, and her whole body quivered. The male circled her frantically on a bloody foot.

Harlin remembered a story he'd heard about a man who was almost beaten to death by a female goose because he got too close to her eggs. He respected that kind of loyalty, and wished his wives were like that. And now he respected the ferocious stupidity of the gander's defense, how he tried to flap his wings menacingly, even as he leaned to one side.

Janet knelt down to get a better look at the birds. Then she got up and went back to the car and returned with Cyrus's gun.

"It's nature, Janet," Cyrus said. "You have to let it take care of it in its own way."

"They mate for life," she said. "He won't leave her, and she's dying. If you leave them here, he'll get hit by another car, and she's going to bleed to death either way."

When she shot the dying goose, the gander went entirely still, out of shock, Harlin guessed, or maybe grief. He remembered a story Grace had told him about a time she watched her father and brother try to birth a calf that was too big. The birth was long and difficult, and they'd had to cut the cow open to get her calf out. Neither of them knew how to sew her up right, and she lost a lot of blood. She was still bleeding when they were done, but the men were tired and said leave her be, she'd be dead by morning. Grace hadn't been able to stand the thought of that lingering, lonesome death, so she had taken her father's gun and shot the cow herself.

That's how it is, Harlin had thought then. Men shoot things to kill them, women shoot things to save them.

Janet put the gun down and looked like she was about to cry. "He doesn't know I was being kind," she said.

"It's all right, Janet," Cyrus said.

"No, it isn't," she said. "That's something you're always wrong about."

She wrapped the gander in a blanket Cyrus found in the back of the car, and they decided to drive around until they found a pond Cyrus knew about where they could leave him. The bird, still rigid, stuck his neck out as if he had been struck by lightning. Janet held him on her lap like a banjo while Cyrus got in on the other side, the gander's head fitting stiffly behind his neck.

A soft rain began to fall. Cyrus turned on a side road and Harlin thought he saw a truck like Jimmy's pass them from the direction of the bowling alley.

In the front seat, Janet was talking to the gander in a low voice and trying to smooth its feathers.

Cyrus was looking for his pond. "Here," he said. "No, wait a minute, that's not the right barn."

"Haven't you ever heard of a street sign?" said Janet. "'Oh, you'll see a stack of hay at the corner of two roads, and if there's some pebbles there, that's where you turn'."

"It's called emotional intelligence," Cyrus said. "You should get some."

Cyrus took a few more turns. The goose began to drool.

"Is that thing bleeding?" Cyrus said. "Something's dripping down my neck."

"It's drool," Harlin said. "They do that when they're scared." He had seen this once on the Discovery Channel. Someone had shot a goose in the head with an arrow, and it turned out that a goose's brain is smaller than its brain cavity, so there was room for the arrow to go through its head and not do any damage. They showed a picture of the goose, swimming around in a pond with an arrow in its head, drooling, and all the other geese moving away from it. In the end they had shot the goose with a tranquilizer and a vet had extracted the arrow and saved the goose and then all the people in the housing development had stood around cheering.

Cyrus put his hand on Janet's leg and Janet tried to swat at him with the arm she had around the goose. The goose came to life and bit Cyrus on the back of his neck. Cyrus swerved, and the car went off the road. Harlin hit the back of the seat and Janet let go of the bird, which started thrashing about, either in rage or in panic. Harlin opened the car door and rolled out, and the goose scrambled past him.

Harlin lay there, watching it go. It had scratched one of his arms and probably bruised his ribs with its powerful wings. Cyrus was on the other side of the car, dazed, and Janet was a few feet away from him, holding her head and laughing.

In the bushes Harlin could hear the goose making a low, keening sound, like mourning. He felt the dirt on his back through his thin shirt and a dull ache below his kidneys. The rain had stopped, but the air was still wet. The evening was fading, and he could hear peepers begin their high-pitched night songs.

"Oh, Janet," Cyrus said. "Janet. I did a terrible thing."

"Let's go," Janet said. "Before the cops come."

"No," Cyrus said. "I got Nancy pregnant, and then I told her I didn't want another kid."

Janet stopped laughing.

"Why are you telling me this?" she said.

"She wanted to have it, but I couldn't stand it. I just couldn't go through that again."

Still lying down, Harlin watched as Cyrus ran his hand through his hair, and Janet sat down next to him, absently running her hands over the pebbles on the ground. The brush where the goose had disappeared had gone still.

"I'm sorry," Cyrus said, "I'm so sorry."

"You're *stupid*," Janet said. "You're so, so stupid."

No one said anything for a while when they got back in the car and on the road. Cyrus drove toward town, and Harlin figured they'd go back to Lucy's like they always did. He'd get drunk and wait for Grace to come in, which she probably would, and he'd be glad to see her. Then he'd tell her that he'd seen Jimmy's truck and if she wanted to hang out with some scum-bag like Slocum, then fine, Jimmy could have her, he didn't care if she lived or died. And then maybe he'd sleep with Linda Hartley, just to show Grace that she shouldn't treat people the way she did.

In the front seat, Janet began to sing a song about a woman who kicked out her husband's windshield, hit him over the head, and chased him out of town for dancing with another woman.

"You have a pretty voice, Janet," Cyrus said. He put his arm around her, his fingers touching the side of her breast. Janet slapped his hand. "I mean it," Cyrus said. "Dick's a lucky man."

"Dan, you moron," Janet said, but when Cyrus moved his hand to her knee, she let it rest there.

It occurred to Harlin that a goose with a hole in its head big enough to shoot an arrow through was better at mating for life than anyone in this car, and he said as much out loud. Cyrus told him to shut up and then pointed an old farmhouse out to Janet.

"Look. See that house?" he said. "That's the one. I pick that one for you."

"That's hideous," Janet said. "You don't know me at all."

Harlin looked out the window at the lake and the hills, the woods where his father used to go round up cattle in the fall. They drove past a cow pasture with a pond, and he saw a group of geese take flight. One by one, they flew into the sky, calling to each other in their haunting, familiar way. Harlin rolled down the window and breathed in the spicy, almost fall wind, listening to their cries going round and round, endlessly into the night.

They did end up at Lucy's, like they always did. Janet slid onto a seat next to her drinking friend of many years, Alice, and happily began to bad-mouth Cyrus.

Cyrus challenged Stewart Levine, a former Navy Seal who lived with his mother, to a game of darts. Harlin called Grace, and when she didn't answer he listened to an old message on the answering machine she'd left when she wasn't mad at him. That made him nostalgic, so he called home again and left a message saying he was sorry and that she should meet him down at Lucy's.

And so he was sitting there, waiting for Grace, when Linda Hartley put a Hank Williams song on the jukebox. She was wearing a pencil skirt and a prim, fitted blouse, a look so irresistible that Harlin asked her to dance, and Linda, who was mad at her boyfriend, a vegetable farmer named Austin, said she'd be honored.

They didn't dance well together. Harlin was trying to two-step and Linda was doing something else, so mostly they banged into each other. But toward the end of the song Linda stumbled into him, and Harlin smelled her skin, a mix of sweat, perfume, and cigarettes that he liked. He put both his hands on her waist, in that soft space between the end of her rib cage and her hips, and pulled her a little closer. Linda let him, but when the song was over she thanked him rather formally and tottered back to her seat at the bar.

Harlin went to the bathroom, which was empty except for him, and stood at the sink. He could hear the muffled sounds of the bar outside, of people calling to each other in their rough and noisy ways. He thought of the gander they'd left in the bushes and wondered if he was still there mourning his mate or if he'd found his way back to his own flock. He'll be all right, Harlin thought. He'll find someone else to fly south with.

There was a sign by the sink that said "Pls. Don't steal the soap. Thx, mgmt." Harlin, who never liked being told what to do, took the soap and put it in his pocket. He caught his reflection in the mirror and looked at his face. He stared at that face, its sunburnt skin, its deepening lines, and wondered if anyone still thought he was handsome.

Snow Fever

Madeline Harris appeared out of nowhere in the late fall, when the sky was damp and gray and depression came drifting in for the winter. She just showed up at Lucy's Tavern one night, a medium-size woman with a long brown braid and a perfect throw. The first time Bill Kane saw her, she beat his boss, Hank, three times in a row at darts. Bill watched this with interest, partly because Madeline was good-looking, and partly because Hank owned the diner where Bill cooked and made pies and Bill liked to see Hank lose.

"She has a good arm," said Hank, sitting down next to Bill after the third game. He had a lean, tough face and sandy-colored hair as fine as a baby's. "I haven't seen that on a woman since I played that mail carrier, Fat Betty."

"I haven't seen that on a man since the last time your mother was in town," said Bill, since Fat Betty was his friend and she was a meter maid, not a mail carrier. Then he changed the subject as if he wasn't interested. He had sworn off women since his last girlfriend, Trish, left him for a piano tuner, but because Madeline was new, and because she didn't seem to care if he lived or died, Bill found himself keeping an eye on her.

Over the next few weeks, he learned that she was dating an organic apple farmer from Lodi who had once been arrested for driving his truck home naked. But Bill noticed that Madeline came into the bar alone and left alone. Unlike the other women at Lucy's, she drank her liquor straight and almost never let anyone buy her a drink. After three bourbons she usually left, unless she had to finish a game, in which case she'd start drinking water.

"She drives a school bus over in Moravia," said Rita, who was tending bar and overheard everything. Rita's mother was Greek and her father German, and Rita carried the hybrid beauty that that kind of marriage makes. She had curly, auburn hair, a Roman nose, and eyes as sharp and black as a hawk's. The only child of farmers, she was raised like a boy and could do most things a man could do, including bed women, which she did spectacularly well.

"Nothing but a bunch of retards and rednecks out there," Bill said, since he was from Moravia and could say it without being rude. But he liked the idea of Madeline Harris, her big hands resting on the oversize steering wheel of a school bus, up early in the morning, before husbands and wives started bickering. He imagined the kids on her route: the red hat girl, the crying kid, the family of four melon-headed boys whose father left a deer carcass on the clothesline for the dogs to chew on, the boy who smelled like cows, the two girls who brought their violins on Thursdays. He saw her managing the clutch of the bus with a smooth-toed work boot, taking those kids to school and away from their homes.

"I don't know if she loves her job," Rita said. "She was driving the bus when that eighth grader was busted giving a blow job to another eighth grader."

"I heard about that," Bill said. "On a school bus. What's wrong with these kids?"

"That's what Maddy said," said Rita. "She stopped the bus, got up, pulled the girl off the boy, and took her outside. Then she said, 'Now you listen to me. Never, ever, do that for free.'"

"It's not bad advice," Bill said.

"No," Rita said. "But I think it got her into trouble."

Bill watched Madeline a lot after that.

One Monday in the beginning of December, Hank closed the diner early and he and Bill went to Lucy's because they were tired and wanted to be drunk. It was three-thirty in the afternoon, and the place was almost empty. They sat at the bar, talking about people they hated (cops, the mayor, Rita, who had cut them off the night before) and women they thought would be hot in bed (Rita, Rita's girlfriend Sheila, and the weather girl on Channel 7). They had just started telling dirty jokes when Madeline came in and sat down a few stools away from them, her back straight as a Mormon. She didn't say anything to either one of them and didn't ask Rita for darts. Instead, she asked for bourbon, neat, which she drank quickly. Then she ordered another.

Bill noticed her drinking more than usual and hoped it would make her more friendly. He and Hank swapped a few more jokes, and Hank loudly overused the word "pussy." Normally this wouldn't have bothered Bill, but tonight, with Madeline sitting right there, Hank's crassness was embarrassing, and Bill stopped laughing when Hank got to the one about Little Red Riding Hood.

Madeline didn't seem to care. She was talking to Rita about her apple farmer, who if Bill heard right had left her for someone else two weeks before and had come over that day to pick up the last of his things. "I followed him around like an idiot," Madeline was saying. "'What is her name?' I kept saying. 'What does she do? Do you love her? Do you love her? Do you?'"

Madeline shook her head in disgust, and Rita refilled her glass. Bill guessed it was her fourth.

"I didn't want to ask him that, of course," Madeline said. "I wanted to shoot him with rock salt. But I couldn't stop. 'Yes,' he finally said. 'Yes, I love her. Not you.'"

In the pause that followed, Bill remembered that when his last girlfriend, Trish, left he hadn't said the right thing either. Before she'd gone, he'd said the words a hundred times: "Don't leave me, please don't ever leave me." It was stupid, since things were good then, but he was always drunk when he said it, and he was always embarrassed the next day.

When Trish finally did go, he hadn't said much until she got into the car. Then right before she drove off, he came out and banged on the window on the driver's side. "Hey!" he yelled. "Hey!" When she rolled the window down, her face was so tired, almost old. I did that, he thought, and everything he'd wanted to say caught in his throat. "Well," he finally said. "See you later."

"He was afraid of cows," Madeline was saying. "How can you be a farmer and be afraid of cows?" She turned toward Bill, and as she did he caught a smell from her jacket. It was a clean, spicy smell. Like sage.

"You farm something else," he said. "You farm fruit."

Madeline laughed. It was a low, warm sound, and when he heard it Bill thought, That's how a woman should laugh. Trish had had a laugh like a screech owl.

"That's like being a bus driver and being afraid of the kids," said Hank.

"Right," said Madeline. She took one of his cigarettes without asking, and Hank, in all fairness, tried to look down her shirt. "Except I'm not afraid of the kids."

"Nope," said Hank. "Telling them not to give out free blow jobs is definitely not being afraid of the kids."

"That's not exactly what I said," Madeline said. "I told her to think about herself first. And if she couldn't do that, to wait until she was 30."

"It wasn't bad advice," said Bill.

"It was very good advice," Madeline said. She tried to rest her foot on one of the rungs of the stool but missed and almost lost her balance. Bill caught her arm, which he noticed had biceps like a man's.

"These girls," she muttered. "They think blow jobs are part of making out. They do it like kissing."

Bill nodded and placed the hand that had just touched her on his thigh. He wanted to kiss her himself and curled his fingers into a fist to keep them from touching her.

"Well," Madeline said. "That man was just a drunk anyway."

"Come on, Maddy," said Rita. "Let me call someone to take you home."

Madeline smiled almost sweetly at her drink. "That's nice, Rita," she said. "But exactly who do you think is going to come pick me up?"

Rita didn't say anything, and Bill was about to say, "Me, please," when Madeline said, "Oh, I'm just kidding. I can get home by myself."

She drank half her drink, then steadied herself and walked out the door.

Bill saw Madeline a few times after that at the bar and tried to meet her eye, but each time she looked right past him. Then she disappeared altogether. She probably went back to her boyfriend, he thought, as he looked for her by the dartboard. Who cares, he thought, even though he knew he did, since the only people over there now were Stewart Levine, Martin Pugliese, and Curly Mahoney, who'd earned his nickname from the collection of pubic hairs he kept in his wallet.

Then in late February a snowstorm hit. It started shortly after one, and by three o'clock Bill was on Route 19 pushing slowly toward the diner in his truck, although he had a nagging suspicion that it was a wasted effort. He figured there would be at least a foot of snow on the roads by seven. There would be plows and roadblocks and cops, cops, cops. He tightened his hands on the wheel and uttered some unkind words about the police in town and authority figures in general.

The truck hit some ice and skidded, almost hitting

a guardrail. Bill straightened it out and checked the rearview mirror for spectators. Seeing none, he readjusted the baseball hat he wore for the kitchen and drove on, thinking about the soup he was going to make that night: a mushroom broth with scallions and potatoes.

Bill loved potatoes. Unlike carrots, peas, or peppers—glossy vegetables, with no stamina—potatoes were survivors. When their bodies shriveled, they would send out long shoots: fierce, white eye-arms looking for light. You had to admire a vegetable for that. Potatoes could last for months that way, even in the bottom of a dark kitchen pantry.

This particular recipe was one he'd gotten from his father, a bowlegged Pole who was a cook by trade but really wanted to be a lion tamer. "Sit!" he'd say to the family's dog, who would look hopefully at the door. "Lie down!" Bill's father would say, gesturing with a thick-wristed hand. "You should put that dog to sleep," he'd mutter to his wife, pouring himself a brandy.

"We should put you to sleep," Bill's mother would say, rubbing the dog's ears.

It was Bill's mother, though, not his father, who had taught Bill to love cooking. She'd grown up with seven loud, nosy siblings, and then she'd gotten married and had eight children. She adored the solitude of preparing a meal, where nothing had a voice, only smells and tastes to speak with. She must have seen something of herself in Bill—always trying to get away from his brothers and sisters—because she invited him into her kitchen, teaching him to baste a chicken, to cook celery with beer for a good broth, to check the color and weight of a vegetable for freshness. After a while he learned to find the same refuge in cooking that she did, even as the noise of the diner or his own life roiled around him.

The snow was falling hard when Bill reached the restaurant and saw Hank's sign in the window: "Closed due to increment weather."

Increment weather, Bill thought. What the hell was that? Little bits of snow, little spurts of hail? He fished in his coat lining for a loose cigarette and cupped a bare hand against the wind to light it. Ten miles through the snow on a suspended license, and the restaurant was closed. That lazy son of a bitch Hank, Bill thought. He walked next door and into Lucy's.

The place was almost full, which was unusual for a Tuesday night. Scarves, hats, and mittens lay in piles along the brick walls. Behind the dark wood bar, Rita poured drinks. In front of him, Fat Betty the meter maid sat with Stewart Levine.

Bill saw Hank and Frankie, the busboy, sitting at a table with a bottle of tequila and six lemon rinds nestled limply in the ashtray. Frankie's girlfriend had just had a baby, and since Frankie wasn't usually out, or a hard liquor drinker, Bill wondered if he and his girlfriend had broken up again.

"Good to see you, man!" yelled Hank, who was clearly drunk. He pounded Bill on the back and Bill coughed. Hank was freakishly strong, and rumored to have lasted longer than any other white man in the Seneca Indian sweat lodges—a fact made even more impressive by the metal plate he had in his head.

"You closed the restaurant," Bill said, sitting down heavily.

"The roads are terrible," Hank said. "No one is going to come out in this weather."

"It's a snow night," Frankie said. He was a small man, young and thin, with a hopeful face. "Like a snow day at school, only at night."

"You could have called," Bill said. "Your hands aren't broken."

Hank offered him a shot to make peace, although they all knew Bill would have ended up at the bar, call or no call. Bill opted instead to get a Guinness. He went back up to the bar and waited for Rita's attention.

Stewart Levine, a former Navy Seal, was talking to Fat Betty. "She only charges me three hundred dollars a month, and I can use the TV and the toaster oven. Not too many landladies let you use their toaster oven." He pulled a handkerchief out of the front pocket of his T-shirt and ran it over his scalp, which was as smooth and brown as a horse chestnut. Bill caught a glimpse of the panther Stewart had tattooed on his inner arm. Stewart's torso was covered with tattoos. A python snaked around his back, a fiery sun burned on his chest. All the tattoos were completed and in full color except for one on his shoulder of a young girl alone in a boat being blown out to sea by an angel. "Stewart's sister," Rita had once told Bill. "She drowned when he was twelve." Bill had rarely seen that one. Somehow Stewart always managed to keep it covered.

"I know, Stewart, you told me already," Betty said.

"That's right," said Stewart.

Bill smiled. Stewart used three hopeless, unappealing lines to pick up women. One was that he would have been a concert pianist if his fingers hadn't been so fat, but they were, so instead he became a plumber. Another was that he was a very rich man and had always tipped the hookers well in Vietnam. The third was that his mother rented him a great room.

Bill finally got Rita's attention and ordered a pint. "Bad night out there," Rita said.

"Wouldn't want to be homeless," Bill said, and then, because he hated the way he made small talk, he turned his back to the bar and let the beer settle into his blood like it was coming home. Out of habit he looked at the dartboard, where he saw Madeline taking careful aim, her long dark hair in a braid down her back.

Bill's throat began to burn. All that time getting used to not seeing her, and now here she was, thick-haired and good-boned and beating Curly Mahoney at darts.

He made himself stop staring before she saw him, and turned back toward the bar again. Stewart had gone to the bathroom, and Fat Betty waved a cigarette in his direction. Bill reached for his lighter.

Fat Betty bought Bill a whiskey, and they toasted the storm. From where he was sitting, Bill had a fine view of Madeline, who was now playing Stewart. The whiskey made him kind toward everyone, and for a moment he even forgave Curly for his disgusting collection. He looked at Madeline's face and wondered if she was a woman who nagged. His ex-girlfriend Trish had picked at everything. Try washing a dish once in a while, she'd said. Do you have to buy the expensive juice? You should stop drinking. Please stop drinking. If you don't stop drinking, I will slit my own throat, and then I'll slit yours.

Hank came over to the bar. "Frankie's started a drinking game where you list places you've done it in alphabetical order." He ordered a shot of Jack Daniel's.

Bill looked at Madeline again. Hank noticed.

"Madeline Harris," Hank said.

"What do you think of her?" Bill said.

"Nice ass," Hank said. "Sweet. Sturdy. She has the kind of ass women are always trying to get rid of. Why do they do that?" Hank looked a little sad. "Just when they have something you can grab on to, they start eating some crap like rice cakes."

Bill shrugged. Madeline shot three straight bulls.

"She could knock a man's teeth through his balls with those arms, though." Hank finished his shot and ordered one for Bill.

"Amen to that." Bill finished his pint and began to feel handsome. He looked at Madeline and imagined grabbing on to that thick hair, that sturdy ass, and it was a good feeling. He drank his shot and remembered that Madeline had called her last boyfriend a drunk, and he had a good feeling about that, too. In his experience, women who said they hated drunks went home with them over and over again.

"I'm going to go home with her," he said.

"I'm sure you are, Bill," said Hank.

"I am," Bill said.

Hank laughed. "What, you talk to her once and you think you'll go home with her? That woman won't even let anyone buy her a drink."

Bill didn't say anything, but he put his pint glass firmly down on the bar so that it made a small, definite warning sound.

"Bill, you barely even talk," Hank said. "What are you going to say? What are you going to talk to her about?"

"Potatoes." Bill said this by accident, which made him mad at Hank.

"Potatoes," Hank said. "Good one. You'd have better luck getting Rita to switch sides."

Bill stood up and considered punching Hank in

the face. Hank knew it and wouldn't have minded hitting him back, so they faced each other, staring each other down.

Then Hank started to laugh. "Potatoes," he said, swatting Bill on the arm. "You're a jackass."

Bill said nothing and walked off to the bathroom.

Outside the snow fell and fell. It silenced the streets, covered driveways, softened cornfields and pastures. Inside the bar, the crowd grew and began to get a little more rowdy.

A little before midnight the power went out. For a few moments everyone was still, hushed by warm darkness. Rita lit some candles, and a few people moved toward the door to leave, but then Stewart sat down at the piano and began banging out some kind of an old rumba. He growled at his clumsy fingers, which sometimes landed on the wrong keys. Hank started heckling him. Stewart played louder until his fingers obeyed and Fat Betty began to dance. She danced slowly at first, her plump hands kneading the smoky air like the tentacles of a sea anemone. She closed her eyes, and as the music picked up, she swung her hips and began to take small, elegant steps. Hank clapped, and Frankie stood up in front of her, swiveling his own hips in time. Madeline stopped her game by the dartboard to watch, her shoulders moving slightly. Fat Betty and Frankie circled each other, and then Frankie reached for her waist and Fat Betty was stuck to his side, dwarfing him with her giant bosom. Bill watched them, a little jealous of Frankie. When Frankie drank too much, he'd sing and dance with anyone. When Bill drank too much, he'd call his own mother a son of a bitch or hit people he wanted to like.

Hank ordered more shots and sang a ballad about a woman who spent most of her life at a bar until she fell down and died there.

Snow fever, Bill thought, watching Frankie's small hands caress Fat Betty's bottom. This whole place has snow fever. He tried to tell Rita about it, but it came out sounding like "cleaver" and Rita asked him if he was going to throw up.

"Oh, don't feel bad," Hank was saying. "She probably died in her sleep."

Bill sat back and let the room grow thick and liquid around him. When the music stopped, Frankie brought out a deck of cards and tried to convince Hank to play. Fat Betty drank some vodka and began to long for past loves. Stewart came back to the bar and put his big head down for a rest.

At midnight Hank stumbled home, and Frankie made his way to the pay phone to call his girlfriend. Madeline finished her last game of darts and came over to the bar to settle up with Rita. She stood about two feet from Bill, but if she noticed him, she didn't let on. Bill tried to think of something to talk to her about—darts maybe, or her ex-boyfriend, or this unexpected storm.

Madeline leaned forward to get Rita's attention, and Bill got a whiff of her clean scent. He noticed a scar, a little half-moon on her cheek. He thought of all the times just one or two words, "please" or "you're pretty," would have changed everything, and how he could never say them when he needed to. He thought about how this was going to happen again, right now, and how stupid that was. And then, because he couldn't stand to watch the moment pass, he did something that surprised even him. He reached out and put his palm on her head and touched her hair.

Madeline didn't move but watched him in the mirror behind the bar. He ran his fingers along her temple and then tucked a loose tendril of hair behind her ear, and for a moment they stayed there, his hand in her hair, her money on the bar.

Then she leaned toward him, just slightly. He moved his hand down the nape of her neck and felt the dampness caused by sweat where the braid began.

Rita came over and picked up her money. Madeline straightened, and Bill's hand dropped to his side. Madeline turned to look at him then, her even gaze meeting his squarely. She looked at him as if to say, Okay. This is it. This is what I'm bringing to the table. Bill thought about what he had to offer: his basement apartment, his bed with dirty sheets, the hole in the ceiling in the living room above the television. He thought briefly of the mechanics of undressing this woman after drinking so much beer. He returned Madeline's gaze, but he must have seemed helpless, or apologetic, or even mean, because she just said, "Okay then. See you later."

Then she put on her scarf, stepped around him, and walked out into the snow.

Bill watched the door shut behind her. In the background Frankie was yelling into the pay phone: "You listen to me! I'm the one talking! Please don't hang up!" Frankie got off the phone and sat down next to Bill where Madeline had been. "Shit," he said. "My ex-girlfriend wants to be my wife. Can you believe that?"

Bill looked at him. Frankie's face bobbed slowly, a little white moon lost at sea.

"I'm only twenty-three," Frankie said. "I'm just getting used to being a father. I don't know if I'm ready to be a husband."

Bill picked up his drink, and as he caught their reflections in the mirror behind the bar—him with his beer, Frankie staring into the remains of his milky White Russian—he thought about that door shutting behind Madeline. He imagined a hundred doors shutting on an endless line of women, all beautiful, all walking away from him into the snow, all chances he had missed and would continue to miss, because women were smart and he was an idiot and at thirty-two years old he still didn't know how to talk to them.

"The hell with it," he said out loud, only his heavy tongue mangled the words and Frankie misunderstood.

"No, the hell with you, man," Frankie said. "The hell with *you.*"

Bill watched him put on his coat and stumble out into the storm. He ordered another pint, and his anger turned to shame.

At about one o'clock, the snow finally stopped and the moon came out. It lightened the sky and turned the pastures and cornfields a soft, pale blue. At the bar, the lights came on. Near the cash register, Stewart began to snore, and Bill decided it was time to go home. He closed one eye and let the jukebox, the bar, and Stewart's big sleeping baby face come into focus. He put on his hat and made his way to the door.

Outside, the air was cold and still. Bill started to turn left, toward his car, but the thought of going home to his empty apartment just seemed too grim. So instead he turned right and slogged back to Hank's restaurant, which would at least be warm. When he got there, he jimmied the lock on the back door and broke in. He stood for a moment in the kitchen, letting the smells of disinfectant, rubber, and steel sink into his skin. He looked at the knives, pots, and pans waiting for him, still and eager as church folk. He imagined that this was how Madeline felt, looking out at her empty bus every morning, before the children got on and started doing unspeakable things.

Perhaps it was the thought of Madeline on her bus, or maybe it was expectancy he felt in the silent kitchen, but Bill made his way to the walk-in cooler.

He took out onions, tomatoes, potatoes, greens, and all of Hank's precious seafood. He took off his coat and put on an apron. Then he went to work.

Bill chopped, boiled, diced, and minced. He laid out the carrots, onions, scallions, and seafood in four careful stacks. He deveined the shrimp, peeling away their translucent skin. He breathed in fresh parsley and thought of Maddy's hair. He chopped vegetables, squeezed tomato juice, and peeled potatoes.

He was opening a clam when he slipped and cut his finger with a kitchen knife. He was drunk enough that it didn't hurt, but it did bleed, so he bashed around the kitchen until he found some duct tape and stopped the blood. Then he went on boiling, chopping, dicing, and tasting, thinking and dreaming of Maddy.

The hours went by and the kitchen grew full and steamy. The smell of Bill's soup grew until it was too big for the kitchen. Bill imagined it trickling out, slowly at first, then gaining force and tumbling into the night sky. He saw it pass the bar, where Rita was putting chairs on tables. He imagined it wrapping around Stewart, who was standing on the street corner, bellowing to anyone who would listen that he was a star in Vietnam, a star, ask anyone. Ask the ladies. It roared and it laughed, and it wafted by

Frankie, sitting at home, smoking a cigarette, wondering if he could be the right husband for his son's mother. Finally it found Madeline Harris, in her house flanked by cornfields and dairy farms, and let her know that Bill knew as well as she did what it was like to come and go places alone.

A week later Bill saw Madeline again. He was on his way to the grocery store to pick up some winter vegetables, and Madeline was walking toward him on the street. Their eyes met, and he wondered if she'd heard about how he'd broken into the restaurant to make some soup, cut open his finger, and then passed out on the rubber matting by the sink, leaving the walk-in cooler open and twenty pounds of fresh seafood out on the counter to spoil.

Maybe if he'd been at Lucy's, on his first or second drink, he would have joked about how he'd made the best soup he'd ever made that night. That it was too bad he couldn't remember how he did it. He might have shown her his stitches. And he imagined that, in the right mood, he might have asked her if she wanted to go home with him, or at least go out for a beer.

But it was daytime. The sun was out and the rules were different. He dropped his eyes and they passed each other without speaking, the way people who drink at the same place often do once they step out of the bar and into the world.

Newspaper Clipping

According to the newspaper, three crimes were committed the night of March 13: Someone stole some bath mats from the girls' shower at the community college, someone else stole the cutout waiter from the front of the grocery store, and Harlin Wilder, his twin brother Cyrus, and their friend Curly Mahoney were arrested for stealing a seven-dollar box of chicken wings from a delivery girl.

This wave of ridiculous crimes was perhaps to be expected. People are crazy by March in that part of the world. All winter they've been stuck inside, sniping at each other and eating canned produce until they can no longer stand the smell of each other's skin. They crave warm sun and longer days. They want to fill their lungs with air that teems with pollen and birdsongs. They want it so much that as soon as April comes and the temperature creeps up to sixty-five, the women who run the apple farm north of town strip to the waist and farm half naked along with their hired men. That's what winter does to people in those parts.

The bath mats were returned anonymously a few days later, and who stole the cutout waiter from the grocery store was no real mystery to begin with. The waiter looked almost exactly like Grace Meyers's ex-husband, and she had already told everyone at Lucy's that if she had to look at that man one more time on her way to get cigarettes and Lean Cuisine she'd shoot the manager of the store with her own gun. In fact, when asked point-blank by Linda Hartley if she'd taken it, Grace said, "Yes. And then I burned it." She had already put a note in the suggestion box asking them to please get rid of that thing, and if they didn't know anything about customer service, she couldn't help them.

Grace was good-looking enough that she could get away with a little petty theft, and that was that. But Harlin's case was a little harder to forgive, since at forty-eight he had outlived his days as a beautiful young man, and he had an impressive police record on top of that.

The summary of his crime would appear in the newspaper the following day and would go like this:

Food theft results in chemical spray.

A late evening skirmish over a food item resulted in three arrests after a box of chicken wings was taken from a delivery woman at around 11:00 P.M.

According to police, a delivery person flagged down an officer and reported the theft of a box of chicken wings from her car after an attempted delivery at the apartment building at 307 W. Chestnut St.

The deliverer said that someone from the apartment building ordered some food, but when it was delivered refused to pay for the item ordered. While she was at the door asking for money, one of the residents of the apartment exited the building, drove her car up the block and took one of the food items left on the front side passenger seat. When the delivery woman saw the resident crossing his backyard with a box of chicken wings from her car and demanded he return them, the resident said he was "just getting takeout." When she attempted to pursue the resident, he climbed a tree and began to consume the stolen goods in an intimidating and rapid manner. All of the people involved, according to the deliverer, seemed incoherent and intoxicated.

Knocks on the apartment door by responding officers were greeted with loud obscenities and demands to see a search warrant. When the door was opened, the residents continued to berate the officers with some jabbing their fingers toward the officers' faces.

Chemical spray was used when the group began circling the officers and one resident, wearing a weight belt and what appeared to be a hat made of crushed beer cans, threatened to set an officer's hair on fire. Backup officers were also called.

Harlin Wilder, 43, and Cyrus Wilder, 43, were charged with second degree obstruction of governmental administration and Class A misdemeanors. Angus Mahoney, 42, was also charged with larceny and auto theft. All three were taken into custody for questioning.

Cyrus Wilder was later to say that the whole thing was a pack of lies. Curly Mahoney simply left town. Only Harlin would admit that yes, in fact, there was some finger-pointing and circling, and someone may have climbed a tree and said something he thought was clever about takeout. ("That's right. I *took* them *out* of your car," he might have said. "That's why they call it takeout.") And someone else may have threatened to set Dale Overstrum's hair on fire, but Dale was an asshole and everyone in town knew it and he probably had it coming. Still, none of this was done by Harlin, who was upstairs trying to sleep at the time, any more than the actual theft of the wings was done by him. And the fact that he was arrested, pepper-sprayed and taken to jail in his bathrobe and slippers with those two morons for a crime he didn't commit was nothing unusual in this stupid town.

LOVE HIM, PETALUMA

On Good Friday, the day she suggested the Easter Parade, Linda Hartley was following advice she had given a reader from Petaluma, California, in one of her recent columns. "We should all wear bonnets," she said to the three men sitting next to her at the bar, "and walk up and down this block." She waved her arm grandly toward the street outside. It was six o'clock, well into happy hour, and Linda was quite a bit drunk.

Linda was often drunk. She lived in a drafty old house two blocks from her bar, Lucy's, with a black cat who bit people. "Nice kitty," she would say to the cat, whose name was Walter, when he tried to take a chunk out of someone's arm. Or sometimes, "If you do that again, you little monster, I'll have a kitty liver sandwich for lunch."

All day Linda sat in her house at a desk littered with Post-it notes, sipping from half-drunk cups of cold coffee, dispensing tidy advice to troubled souls she'd never met. "You are much better off being alone than with someone who makes you miserable," she told the adolescent readers of *Sugar and Spice* (1.5 million subscribers). "If he says something that makes you jealous, make a joke out of it," she told the slightly older readers of *Woman Today* (2 million subscribers, including dentists). "Don't cause a scene or tell him you want to have a talk. Men hate to hear they have to have a talk."

Not that she followed her own advice. Linda had been known to talk a man's ear off and had once been asked to leave Lucy's after she called another woman a dirty shit fly for flirting with her boyfriend. Still, she had high hopes for her readers, whom she imagined to be flat-faced and openmouthed, insatiable as baby starlings. Her columns were very popular, and she made a lot of money writing them.

The advice she had given Petaluma, of course, had nothing to do with bonnets but rather with various ways to distract oneself from a broken heart.

"Dear Ms. Hartley," Petaluma had written. "I just broke up with my boyfriend of a year. I know it was the right thing to do, as he might have cheated on me, and he drinks a lot. I know these are bad things, and I knew that if I loved myself I'd have to leave him. But all I do is want him back. Maybe I was too cold the last time and I could make it better this time. Maybe I should call him. Do you think I should call him? Please Help."

"I'm sorry, but I'd have to say no calling," Linda had advised. "If you think he cheated on you, he probably did. Stay busy. Start a special project, like gardening or wine tasting. Or try a fitness class, like African dance. Once you develop your own interests, you might find it easier to let him go. After all, there are plenty of fish in the sea."

It wasn't a bad answer, Linda thought, although she was still stuck on one particular fish, a vegetable farmer named Austin. In the same way that Linda nurtured her troubled souls, Austin cared for beans and cabbages, feeding them with water and nitrogenized dirt and pulling bugs off their leaves and stems with his careful hands. After a day of driving tractors, tending corn, and building towers from dirt for the potatoes to grow in, he came to Lucy's for seven to fifteen Budweisers. Sometimes he got feisty and arm-wrestled Rita, and other times, if the music was right, he'd get loose and charming. Then Austin would start to dance.

That's how Linda fell in love with him. One night in late May, when the cherry trees bloomed hopefully under the moon, she stuck her hips to his and just danced, a half-smoked cigarette dangling from her fingertips, until two in the morning.

They danced pretty well together, if you asked her. They danced in bars, outside in the park, and one night, after they drank two bottles of whiskey, they danced naked in her big, drafty house, two drunk fools knocking against each other, making moon-shadows on the floor.

It wasn't until the wheat fields turned purple and summer began to die that Linda noticed how many things Austin broke when he danced. In September he fell into a table at Lucy's and broke four wine-glasses. In October he broke a pitcher of beer, a candy dish, and two pint glasses. At her Christmas party in December he danced on her cat and almost broke Walter's tail. Linda suggested that he dance before drinking ten bottles of Budweiser and a half a bottle of whiskey, and he advised her not to nag.

Then in February, while the wheat seeds slept peacefully beneath the snow, Austin danced a mambo with a pretty girl who liked to drink even more than he did and broke Linda's heart.

"Goddammit," she said, and told him it was over. But then he showed up on her doorstep at midnight a week later and she let him in. And when he told her he loved her, not the other girl, she was so relieved she took off all her clothes. "We're not back together though," she said. "Not until you stop drinking."

"You're so pretty," he said, and Linda let him stay over the next night, too.

Earlier in the week, before Good Friday, Austin had called her to see if she'd go with him to visit his family in Maine for Easter. "No," Linda said. "We are broken up," she said, even though she wanted more than anything to get into the car and drive for miles with him, with his hand on her leg, the way they'd done all summer back when things were good and she hadn't cared about his reckless nature or how gray his skin was for a twenty-seven-year-old boy. "I can't go," she sighed, because she also knew that if she did, she'd have to lie to her therapist. Again. "Anyway, it's over," she told herself after Austin hung up the phone.

Now it was Good Friday and a good day for listening to good advice. Austin had gone to his family's house without her, and Linda told herself she'd done the right thing. Keep yourself busy, she'd reminded herself as she walked briskly to the bar. ("Always walk as if you are five minutes late for an appointment," she'd advised her readers. "You burn extra calories and exude confidence.") There are plenty of fish in the sea.

"I'm serious," she said to Benny Jackson, one of the happy hour regulars. "We should make our own bonnets and have an Easter parade."

Benny wiped the foam from his third Guinness off of his upper lip. He was a tall, thick man with a handsome nose and yellow eyes. One of his eyes was nearsighted and one was farsighted, which made him fairly good at darts but not so good at walking straight or, for that matter, driving. As a drunk, Linda once told him, Benny was perfect. Almost a natural.

"A parade," he bellowed. He was deaf in his right ear and almost always yelled.

"We could start a tradition," Linda said.

"Where the hell am I going to get a bonnet?"

"You have to make it," Linda said.

"I don't know," Benny said. "I may have to do my taxes on Sunday."

"Oh, bullshit," said Linda, losing patience. "Do them tomorrow. The parade will be at five-thirty," she decided, "which leaves you all day to make your bonnet. You'll do it," she went on. "Come on, I know you will."

Linda thought she knew a lot about Benny, since she'd been drinking with him for more than a year. She knew, for example, that he was a kind man and a good mechanic and not a person in the bar would say otherwise. She knew, from the time she bet him that since he was asthmatic and tone-deaf he wouldn't have the guts to belt out "White Wedding" at a karaoke contest, that he rose to almost any challenge. She knew, because he'd told her, that Benny was divorced, and that he had an eight-year-old son who was sending anonymous notes to his teacher that started with "Dear Stupid." She knew, because she drank with him, that he consumed a six-pack of beer and up to six shots of Maker's Mark a night, unless he had custody of his boy, when he didn't touch a drop, no matter how much the withdrawal made his hands shudder.

"I'll tell you what," Benny said. "If you can get Stewie Levine to sign up, I'll stick some marshmallow chicks on a fishing hat and be in the parade."

Stewart was standing at the end of the bar, well into his second pitcher. A former Navy Seal, he kept his hair short—actually, he was bald, and although the three pitchers a day he drank widened his belly, he stretched his old T-shirts neatly over it and tucked them into his jeans, which he always bought too long and rolled up, as if he might still grow a few inches.

"Oh, Stew, be in the Easter Parade," said Linda.

Stewart looked at her with brown, soggy eyes.

"What, baby?" he said.

"I think we should all make bonnets and parade to the Helmsman," she said.

The Helmsman was a block away from Lucy's. At eleven o'clock, if the college students came down and stunk up Lucy's with cologne and clove cigarettes, Lucy's regulars would trickle over to the Helmsman in a thin, wobbly line, like worker ants coming back from feasting on the queen's nectar. They'd keep drinking and play pool until three or four in the morning. Sometimes they danced or cried, and occasionally they engaged in oral sex in the sixty-five-year-old bathrooms. Linda loved the Helmsman as much as Stewart did. She herself had wept and danced and would have engaged in oral sex in the bathroom, but at the time she and Austin had been too drunk, so they sat on the toilet and shared a few slobbery kisses until Stewart pounded on the door and threatened to kill whoever was in there with his bare hands.

"We'll drink whiskey at the Helmsman," she went on, "and parade back home to Lucy's."

Stewart looked at her red-lipsticked lips and heaved a long, very sad sigh. "I don't have a bonnet," he said.

"You have to make your own," she replied. "Those are the rules."

"Go to hell," Stewart said and followed his barrel belly outside to lie down.

Hank Stevens tried to remember what he had in the diner's lost and found and said he would wear a bathing cap with daisies on it. Elizabeth Teeter, the schoolteacher who was so pretty Hank couldn't stand next to her, said she was going to wear a straw hat loaded with lilacs and edible fruit. She said this with an elegant sweep of her bony arm and carried her drink to the other end of the bar.

"She's so fucking beautiful," Hank sighed. "Isn't she beautiful?"

"She's a beauty, all right," said Benny.

"Beauty," said Linda, who might have been beautiful if it weren't for a slight overbite, "is only skin deep."

Linda had recruited six people to join the parade by the time she wandered back to her house: Benny, Hank, Stewart, Elizabeth, Rita the bartender, and Harlin Wilder. Harlin had recently been arrested because someone in his house had ordered a box of chicken wings and, when it was delivered, grabbed the food and refused to pay, spewing so much foul language that the delivery girl called the police. Four people, including Harlin, were pepper-sprayed as a result of this petty crime, and three people, including Harlin, spent the night in jail.

"It was my roommate, not me, that did it," Harlin told Linda. "I've been trying to stay away from trouble."

"I know, honey," she said. "But maybe you should stop living with your brother."

Linda was in the bathtub the next morning, sipping some coffee and nursing a terrible headache, when she heard her neighbor Dixie approach her door and shove something through the mail slot.

She dried herself off and went out to investigate. Beneath the mail slot was a misdelivered batch of let-

ters, forwarded from one of the magazines in which her columns appeared. Attached to the pack was a handwritten note that said, "If you don't keep that goddamn cat of yours in your own apartment, I'm going to yank its little head off. Love, thy neighbor. (Ha Ha.)"

Linda gave the note to the cat to eat and opened the first letter, which was from Petaluma.

"Dear Ms. Hartley, Thank you for answering my letter in your column," Petaluma wrote in small, curly letters. "I liked your advice. I joined a book club, I signed up for some art lessons, and I even bought a Thighmaster and a fitness tape to do whenever I think of calling my ex-boyfriend. I started to feel a little bit better, but then the other day I saw him with another woman. The thing is, she is tall and beautiful, and I am short and fat. I know I should love myself, and most days I do, but then I see them together, and my legs feel like thick, barky tree trunks. I know he's probably a cheater and I deserve better. But I don't think I should ever have let him go, Ms. Hartley. I'm a full-figured girl who doesn't get a lot of attention in this world. And it's terrible to be alone."

"Oh, Petaluma," Linda said and picked up a pen.

"It is hard to be alone," she wrote back gently. "But it's better than being with someone who won't love you the way you deserve. Make a list of things you like about yourself," she wrote. "Keep the list and recite it to yourself every time you see him with this woman."

A therapist had given Linda this trick after she broke up with Liam, the man she'd loved before Austin. When Liam broke up with her to get back together with his old girlfriend, Linda had made up a list of things she liked about herself in case she ever ran into them. "I have very strong legs," she had written. "I can sing. I have great skin for a woman over thirty. I can read maps. I have never been in jail." But she never had to use her list, because she'd left town, where Liam lived, and moved up north to her drafty house near Lucy's.

"It is not a question of him finding someone better than you," Linda continued writing to Petaluma. "It is a question of people being suitable for one another. He is not suitable for you, and you are not suitable for him. You'll find someone who is much better, don't worry. In the meantime, use that list."

She looked at her words. "Right, Walter?" she said

out loud to the cat, who had settled himself on her desk. "It's not rejection, it's suitability. Just like Austin is not suitable for me, and I am not suitable for him." Walter tilted his head and looked hungrily at her thumb. "No, sweetie pie," she said, pulling him up on her lap. "No biting."

She put Petaluma's letter aside and picked up the next one in the packet.

"My boyfriend and I were dry-humping on the couch and his penis got inside my vagina. Could I be pregnat? P.S.: Dry-humping is when you go through the motions of doing it, but you keep all your clothes on anyway. Love, Wondering."

"Oh, dear, confused Wondering." Linda sighed and stuck a Post-it note to the top of Wondering's letter. "Thx for clarification," she wrote. "Explain pre-ejaculatory fluids."

She paused for a moment and looked out the window. "Although, really, thanks for nothing," she said to the cat. "I mean, what makes her think I don't know about dry-humping? I could dry-hump my way through Cuba if I felt like it. She can't even spell 'pregnant.'"

Walter chewed happily on a spider. Linda added a splash of bourbon to her coffee.

The next letter was from a woman in Knoxville who was upset with her fiancé. "He says I hold my knife and fork like a child!!" Knoxville wrote. "I am certainly willing to take criticism, and I know marriage is all about compromise. Still, I don't think 'You hold your cutlery like an infant' is a nice thing to say."

"You are right to be concerned," Linda wrote. "Don't marry him." She looked at her words and pulled off another Post-it. "Make a list of things you don't like about HIM," she wrote and stuck it to the top of Petaluma's letter.

Linda decided that was enough work for a Saturday morning and it was time to focus on her parade. In the back of her closet she found a sombrero she'd won at Lucy's for kissing Rita on the lips. It was orange and had a turquoise band around it with the words "La Cuervoracha!!" Fine, she thought and left the house to go find some more decorations.

At the dollar store she bought four fake red lilies the size of soup bowls; a basket of plastic grapes, bananas, and apples; and some polyester yellow roses. In the gardening section of the hardware store she found a battery-powered bluebird that sang "Toowhee! Toowhee!" if jostled.

On her way home she ran into Benny, who was on his crooked way to the bar.

"I thought you were working on your taxes today," Linda said.

"I didn't say I'd be in that parade," Benny said, eyeing the red lilies sticking out of the top of one of her bags. "I didn't say I wouldn't, but I didn't say I would either."

"I think you should buy me a drink," Linda said and followed him into the bar.

Stewart Levine and Harlin Wilder were already there, talking about Martin Pugliese, who had just gotten arrested for pulling a shotgun on his own son.

"You ever seen his kid?" Stewart was saying. "You'd pull a gun on him, too, if that monster came running at you."

"I might," said Harlin. "But I'm not a big guy. Martin, on the other hand, is pretty big."

Stewart couldn't argue with that.

Benny bought Linda a shot of tequila, and Harlin moved over one stool so she could sit down.

"Linda Hartley," Harlin said. He raised a half-drunk bottle of Schaefer. "Miss Lonely Hartley," he went on. "Linda, I'd like to buy you a drink," he said.

"How's your girlfriend, Harlin?" Linda said.

"My girlfriend's fine."

"We're all fine," said Benny, and Linda raised her glass to him.

Harlin looked at Linda's bag. "How's your bonnet, Linda?" he said.

"In the works," Linda said.

Harlin shook his head. "That's a crazy idea you have there," he said.

"Maybe." Linda smiled.

"Harlin's got ideas," said Stewart. "Stealing chicken wings from a delivery girl isn't a bad idea."

"Unless you end up in jail," said Benny.

"Now listen, you two. Harlin says he didn't do it," Linda said.

"Let me ask you something, Linda," said Harlin. "Why won't you let me buy you a drink?"

"I have a drink."

"You do have a drink. But even if you didn't have a drink you wouldn't let me buy you one."

"Someday you can buy me a drink."

"Naw," Harlin went on. "You know what I mean, Benny? I mean, here's an intelligent, good-looking woman sitting right next to us. And for months she goes out with the biggest tomcatter in town."

"We're broken up," Linda said.

"And I can't even buy her a drink."

"I wouldn't call him the biggest tomcatter in town," Linda said.

"More like a tomkitten," said Benny. He repositioned himself to the side of Linda so that he was almost between her and Harlin. It was a protective move, and Linda leaned toward him slightly to let him know she noticed.

"What is it about that guy?" Harlin pulled out a cigarette and lit it with fingers that were red and chapped from working outside on a road crew all fall and winter. "The women around here can't get enough of him."

Linda waved the smoke away from her face and wrapped her napkin around the base of her shot glass. She thought about trying to explain to Harlin how she loved Austin in spite of herself, how his sweet words and devastating sadness made her feel reckless and kind. But when she looked at Harlin, his jaw was set.

"Harlin," she said. "Remember Grace? We all knew she was no good. Every time you came in here you were mad at her. Remember how she drove your new truck to Interlaken when she was drunk and came back with Robbie Nathan's phone number tucked into her bra?"

Harlin pulled a plastic sword out of the garnish tray on the bar and carefully cleaned the space between his two front teeth.

"And remember the night you caught her making out with your friend Richie and you got so mad you smashed his head into a street sign, and he got back up and almost killed you?"

"I remember that," said Benny. "He was a little guy, too."

"He was so coked up, he bounced back three times," said Harlin. "I've never seen anything like it. He knocked me down twice before he finally collapsed."

They all sat still for a minute, giving Richie's addiction a moment of silence. Then Linda continued.

"I bet every time you saw Grace you knew somewhere that the whole thing between you two was doomed," she said. "And I bet that made your heart ache so much you didn't know what you'd do next." Linda made a helpless gesture with her hands, and Harlin put his plastic sword down.

"That's what it was like with me and Austin," she said.

Harlin stared at her hard for a minute, as if seeing her with a new pair of eyes. Then he shrugged and went back to his drink.

"Well, I knew it was something," he said. "I mean, the women around here can't get enough of him."

Linda had heard the comment the first time and for a second imagined shoving a big red lily up Harlin's ass.

"See that?" Linda said. "You see that? That is exactly why I won't let you buy me a drink."

Harlin glared at her and put his dollar down on the bar. He finished his beer and walked out.

Linda ordered another tequila and drank it while Benny stayed next to her, watching Stewart try to beat himself at darts.

"The thing is," Linda said after a while, "people don't really want good advice. Good advice is: Eat bananas. Use condoms. Break up with the beautiful, terrible woman who will never stay with you. Bad advice is: Drink three bourbons a day. Sleep with your ex-boyfriend. Go look for a husband in a bar."

"That's the good stuff," said Benny, pulling a cigarette out of a pack someone had left on the bar. Linda watched him pull a cloud of unfiltered smoke into his asthmatic lungs. It occurred to her, not for the first time, that in spite of the fact that he was a good-looking man and made a decent living as a mechanic, she had never seen Benny leave the bar with a woman. In fact, she'd never seen Benny with a woman, period, except Rita, maybe, or herself.

"Benny," she said. Benny nodded, his eyes still on Stewart, who was muttering vague threats at the side of himself that was winning. "Are you still in love with your ex-wife?"

Benny didn't look at her, and the question hung there in the thick air between them. It sat there for so long that Linda had to double-check to make sure she wasn't sitting next to his deaf ear.

"That's not really your business," he finally said.

It was the first time that he had refused her anything, so she did not say what she thought, which was that it *was* her business. In fact, other people's sadness was exactly what her business was. Only really, what could she do about it? She could barely live with her own.

"Benny," she said, putting a hand on his arm, "don't mind me." She gathered up her bags and paid for her drink. "I'm just drunk," she said and made her way home.

That night Linda sat alone in her drafty house, weaving flowers, plastic fruit, and ribbons onto her sombrero. There were no drunken messages from Austin on her machine when she got home, and the phone didn't ring at one, two, or three in the morning. "Stay busy," she reminded herself. "There are plenty of fish in the sea."

The morning of the Easter Parade, Linda decided to make a few calls to remind people that it was happening. By noon it was not going well. Rita's girlfriend had found out about a one-night stand she had had with a man, and they were involved in an all-day fight. Hank had no idea what fool business she was talking about, but anyway, he had to fumigate the kitchen at the diner. Elizabeth Teeter was grading papers. "No one will come to my parade," sighed Linda. She thought about calling Stewart, but calling his mother's house made her nervous. She thought about calling Harlin, but she was still a little annoyed with him from the day before. She thought about calling her therapist but decided to fix herself a vodka tonic instead. That one tasted good, so she had a few more.

At five-thirty, the estimated time of the parade, Linda was feeling much better. She added some finishing touches to her bonnet and then stepped back to admire her work. La Cuervoracha!! was transformed. Plastic apples, bananas, and the huge red lilies covered its brim. In the middle of the front, perched on top of an obscene pile of grapes, was the battery-powered bluebird, ready to sing.

"This," she told Walter, "is one hell of a bonnet."

She put on a pink dress and some high heels and, balancing her bonnet carefully on her head, strode briskly to Lucy's as if she were five minutes late. I look good, she thought as she caught her reflection in the plate-glass windows of Hank's Diner. "I am fabulous," she assured herself. She caught Hank staring at her from the inside of the diner and waved.

"Jesus Christ, look at that," Hank said. "It looks like someone vomited up Easter on that woman's head." He waved back.

Lucy's was practically empty when Linda entered, and for an instant the vodka gave her a terrible dose of clarity. She *was* the Easter Parade. One drunk woman on a Sunday afternoon wearing a sombrero. With a bird on it.

But then as her eyes adjusted to Lucy's cool, dim interior, she noticed three figures clustered at the end of the bar by the television. Benny, Harlin, and Stewart were on their second round. Benny was holding a hat made out of a piñata, a three-tiered papier-mâché chick bursting out of an egg. It had an open beak and huge blue eyes, and it would add a good two feet to

Benny's already substantial height. Hank had loaned him a box of toothpicks from the diner, and Benny was busy sticking pink marshmallow rabbits on top of the thing's head. When he saw her, Benny held it up to the one intrepid piece of sun that pushed its way through a dirty window above the bathroom door.

"Benny, it's fantastic," said Linda, thinking she might cry.

"I had to borrow my friend Rusty's jabber saw to make it fit on my head," Benny yelled.

Next to Benny, Harlin was also stabbing marshmallow rabbits with toothpicks, which he then stuck to a black fedora through which two pink rabbit ears poked. "I am Peter Cocktail," he said grandly, and Linda held on to her hat and kissed him full on the mouth. Stewart, who was sitting next to Harlin, demanded a kiss himself. He was wearing a pith helmet and was simply stabbing marshmallow rabbits. Onto his helmet he had pasted a piece of paper that said, "My bonnet, love it or leave it."

"Stewart, it's beautiful," she said, patting his shoulder. She looked in the mirror to check her own bonnet, and in its reflection saw Austin standing near the dartboard, wearing a faded green T-shirt that made his eyes bluer than the sea.

Austin smiled and waved, and Linda smiled back, turning to take a step toward him. As she did, the pretty mambo queen came out of the bathroom and made her way toward the empty stool next to Austin. Linda stopped smiling and backed up, bumping into an inflatable parrot that hung from the ceiling from last year's Cinco de Mayo celebration. "Toowhee! Toowhee!" shrieked her bluebird. The mambo queen said something to Austin, and Linda began to recite her list of things she liked about herself. I can read maps, she thought. I have a widely published, reputable column. The girl stood on her tiptoes and kissed Austin's high cheekbone, and Linda watched as his hand snaked around her waist. I can sing, she thought. I can run four miles without stopping on very strong legs. A plastic banana dropped from her bonnet.

"I can get out of this goddamn bar," she said out loud and turned to the three men. "Well, boys," she announced, "let the parade begin."

Linda linked arms with Stewart, Benny, and Harlin, and they marched down the block. "Nice hats," said Fat Betty the meter maid.

"Are those . . . bonnets?" asked a hippie.

"We're the Easter Parade!" bellowed Benny, clocking Linda on the head with a meaty hand.

"Toowhee! Toowhee!" sang her bird.

At the Helmsman, Linda bought Benny and Stewart bourbon and let Harlin buy her a shot of tequila. Harlin saw his lawyer, Lanford Guthrie. "I know you don't like to talk shop when you're off duty," he said, "but I didn't steal the chicken wings. Curly was the one that did it. I was in bed when it happened. They took me to jail in my bathrobe and slippers, for Christ's sake." His ears bobbed up and down when he spoke, and Lanford nodded weakly.

"I believe you," he said.

Harlin clapped him on the back and went to the bathroom.

"Why the hell not," Lanford said to Linda. "I believe all of them. Every time. And you know what? Every time they fucking lie to me."

Stewart ordered himself a pitcher and elbowed his way to the pool table.

"Nice hat," said Frankie, the busboy at Hank's.

"Eat me," growled Stewart, and Frankie let him break.

Linda sat at the bar next to the parole officer and ordered a double bourbon. She had given up thinking about things she liked about herself and had begun listing the men who might love her. "That Liam, he loved me," she said. "Mark Mintner loved me for ten years even though I only kissed him once. Eric Richards and I had very hot sex not even six months ago." She swatted at a bunch of grapes that had come loose and were drooping over her ear.

"I love you, sweetheart," said the bartender. He gave her her bourbon and patted her hand. "We all love you. Really, we do."

Linda gave up on her bonnet and placed it gently on the bar. She sipped her drink and saw Benny at the jukebox picking out music, his chest laboring to pull oxygen into his weary lungs.

Benny saw her staring and came over to offer his hand. "Put on your bonnet, Ms. Hartley," he said. "They're playing our song."

Linda looked up at him—his fine nose and the semicircles of soft lavender skin that underlined his yellow eyes. Benny burped, and his overexcited bonnet wobbled a little. She saw that on one of the bonnet's outstretched wings Benny had stuck a tag that said, "Hello, my name is Benford." Benny, she thought. Benny loves me.

She imagined that, over at Lucy's, Austin was finishing his fifth or sixth beer. He would be starting to move now, getting ready to twirl and spin the other girl until she felt light and important as a late spring. Linda thought of short, full-figured Petaluma squeezing the hell out of her Thighmaster and wishing the phone would ring. We only get pieces of love, she thought. Sometimes that's the best we can do. Oh, love him, Petaluma, she thought. Love him.

She put on her bonnet and took Benny's arm. They walked to the jukebox, which was playing a Willie Nelson version of "Goodnight, Irene." Benny put his thick arms around her, and she pressed her body full-length against his. She pressed into him and he pressed back, and they swayed together for almost an hour. Even after the songs switched to a faster rhythm, they stayed that way, two flowers drifting in the bar's smoky haze, dancing as if they'd been in love for a hundred years.

GRACE

When Harlin Wilder got out of jail for driving drunk and violating probation, he rented a place on the outskirts of town next to Fat Betty, who from the looks of things owned about twenty-five cats.

"Sorry the whole block smells like cat shit," she said to Harlin the day after he moved in. "But with your record you're lucky anyone would give you a lease."

She had wide hips and a sure-footed walk that at another time in his life might have made Harlin want to start something up with her, but when Harlin got out of jail he had promised himself he would live a quieter, more peaceful life. He planned to do this by drinking at home, counting to ten before hitting anyone, and staying away from women, his ex-wife Grace especially, but all other women as well. So he ignored his neighbor's nice ass and the two pairs of thong underwear hanging on her clothesline and said, "Good to see you, Betty."

Betty nodded. "I'll mind my business," she said, "and you mind yours."

"Whatever you say," Harlin said, but she was already on her way back into her house.

At first Harlin lived up to his own expectations. Through his friend Bill Kane, he got a job working construction for Bill's brother, and he spent the rest of the time in his apartment watching TV and crocheting, a skill he'd picked up in jail. Sometimes he'd get out an atlas and plot a trip to a town or city he might like to visit if he ever moved. Other nights he played his banjo and tried not to listen to Fat Betty having loud sex next door.

In November, business died down for the winter and Bill's brother cut back Harlin's hours. Harlin's twin brother Cyrus got kicked out of their sister's house, and Harlin let Cyrus move into the tiny room next to the kitchen. In December, Cyrus started a band called Super Lady and suggested that Martin Pugliese, his keyboardist, move in, too.

"Pugliese?" said Harlin. "I don't trust that guy."

"We could afford cable," Cyrus said.

"He has hips like a girl and a mean baby face," said Harlin.

"Just for a month or so," said Cyrus.

"No one likes a mean baby," said Harlin.

In January, Super Lady began practicing in the living room, and Harlin decided that it wouldn't hurt if he went to a bar to watch TV. And that's how he found himself back at Lucy's Tavern in front of Rita Johnson, the bartender.

"Well, Harlin," she said. "What bad luck brings you in here?" She put a bottle of Utica Club down in front of him.

Harlin smiled. "Good to see you, too, Rita," he said.

"I was wondering when you'd stop in," she said. "It's been a while."

She turned away to get a drink for Bill Kane, who was sitting at the end of the bar making his grocery list. Harlin took a drink, letting the stale air relax him. It was his favorite time of day to be in a bar. Things were quiet and no one was fighting or hustling, and if he needed her, he could have Rita all to himself, or if he didn't, she'd just wash glasses or go down to the basement and stock bottles.

Harlin watched the smoke from his cigarette wind lazily up toward the open window above the bathroom. The smoke was light and slender, and Harlin took a second to enjoy it. It was one of the many things he noticed since he'd gotten out of jail: how smoke looked in a bar, how good sausage and gravy on a biscuit tasted. Once before he'd gone to jail, he'd overheard a social worker at Lucy's talking about how locking people up just made them mean. And Harlin would now argue that yes, maybe the first year made you mean. But after that, what got you was the boredom. There was nothing to do but sit around and think about what you did to get in there, about why you were so alone and how much you missed the things you used to have.

So that's how he was sitting, content, enjoying the things he had, when he heard the door open. Something made him glance up to see who it was, which he almost never did since he hated it when he came into a bar in the daytime and all the gray, work-worn faces turned to look at him like the drinking dead. But this sound made him turn, an instinct he immediately regretted, because there was Grace Meyers, the last person he wanted to have see him drinking in the afternoon.

Grace had cut her hair short so it curled around her face. She put her purse on the bar and pulled out a pack of long, skinny cigarettes.

"Nice haircut, Grace," Rita said, reaching for a bottle of bourbon. She hesitated a second to see if her instinct was right, and Grace nodded.

"Neat," she said.

Harlin wondered if she'd talk to him and wondered what he would say if she didn't. He hadn't seen her since he'd gone to Florida to try to get her back and Jimmy Slocum had answered the door. He'd heard she was back in town. He'd even imagined bumping into her and thought of a few things he might say, like, "Hi, Grace, how's your sister?" or "You still hanging out with that douchebag?" But now that she was sitting right there, he had no idea what to do next.

So it was Grace who finally spoke. "Harlin," she said.

Harlin put his cigarette down. "Grace."

The light from the windows revealed the things about her face Harlin had loved most—her pert mouth, her pale skin. There were some new details, too: two creases deepening from the sides of her mouth to her nose, and lines beneath her eyes. He was struck by how ordinary she looked, and that realization, plus the three bottles of beer he'd already drunk, made him relieved and bighearted.

"Welcome back, Grace," he said.

"Thank you," she said. "I heard you were back, too."

It was nice of her to say it like that, as if he'd just gone someplace warm and sunny for the winter instead of being locked up for a fifth DWI and aggravated assault.

Rita put the bourbon down in front of them, and Harlin pushed the ten-dollar bill he'd put out on the bar toward her. He tried to catch her eye, but Rita was a professional and betrayed no reaction to the meeting that was taking place. She took Harlin's money and moved back to Bill Kane.

"So how've you been?" Grace said.

"Good," he said. "I've been pretty good."

She took out a cigarette, and he lit it.

"I heard you got a job."

He nodded. "Doing some roofing. Trying to live a clean life, you know."

Grace smiled. "How's that going for you?"

"Not too bad." He thought about telling her that, actually, this was the first time he'd been in Lucy's in months, but he didn't want her to think he cared what she thought.

"How's Jimmy?" he asked.

"He married me," Grace shrugged.

"That's right. You're a married woman now."

"Oh shit, Harlin, when haven't I been married?" Grace blew smoke out toward the mirror in front of her and turned back to Harlin. "I even married you at one time."

Harlin laughed and then wrapped his hand around his beer bottle, comforted by its coolness. Grace laughed, too, leaning forward a little as she did. Harlin caught a glimpse of a red bra beneath her shirt. He felt himself slipping dangerously toward longing and motioned to Rita for another drink.

"It's on Bill," Rita said when she came down to their end of the bar. She picked up Grace's empty glass as well. "For both of you."

Grace smiled at Bill and mouthed "Thank you."

Harlin turned around and mouthed "Fuck you" to Bill. Then he took the free drink.

"Don't you work for that guy's brother?" Grace had turned back to Harlin, but not fast enough for him to miss her quick appraisal of Bill.

"Yeah," he said. Out of the corner of his eye, he saw Bill reach behind the bar for the controls to the television.

"He's not a bad-looking guy," Harlin said.

"Don't start," Grace said.

"I'm not starting anything," Harlin said. "I'm just saying that Bill, the guy who got me my job, the guy who just bought you a drink, is a good-looking guy."

"Harlin," she said. She opened her mouth as if she were about to say something and then stopped herself. Then she picked up her purse and her cigarettes.

"I have to go," she said.

Harlin shrugged. "You just got here," he said. He said it with a laugh, as if she were overreacting, but it came out sounding bitter, and he felt like a jerk. He looked at the television. Bill had it on a food show, and Harlin watched a stocky man with a neck as thick as an elephant's foot pour oil into a hot pan and yell "Ka-boom!" which threw his audience into a delighted fit of applause.

Grace drank the rest of her drink and put some money on the bar. Then she said, "Harlin, let me ask you something. How hard would it be just to have a normal conversation with me? Something like 'It's nice to see you, Grace,' or 'Hi, Grace, how's your sister?' That's what normal people say to each other."

Harlin stared at her as coolly as he could.

"No answer?" She made an exasperated sound in the back of her throat and shook her head. "Of course there's no answer."

Rita took Grace's tip, and Harlin finished the rest of his drink.

"Thanks, Rita," Grace said. Rita nodded.

Harlin cleared his throat. "Grace," he said.

She put on her coat.

"You look good."

Grace didn't look at him, but she didn't leave either. She stood there with her jacket on, exhaling smoke and watching her hand grind her cigarette into the ashtray.

"I mean it," Harlin said. "I hope Jimmy makes you happy."

Grace's face softened. "Thank you," she said.

And then, even though he knew better than to invite that woman anywhere, Harlin heard himself say, "Stay out for a drink with me."

"Oh, Harlin," she said.

He just kept looking at her.

She sighed, and the expression on her face was the same as the one she always got after they'd worn themselves out fighting. "I'm not like that anymore," she said.

"No," Harlin said.

They were quiet.

"Me neither," he finally said.

On the way home, Harlin was in a bad mood. Grace Meyers, he thought. Some people you just couldn't be in the same room with. His marriage to that woman had lasted less than six months, and no one knew better than he did that the last thing he should do was take her out for a drink. He was mad at himself for asking, mad because she said no, and he was mad because the first thing she saw when she walked into the bar was him sitting there staring at her like a fool. All of it pissed him off so much that he barked at one of Fat Betty's mangy black cats, who was eating a mouse by his driveway.

"Hey!" Fat Betty yelled from her window. "That cat didn't do anything to you."

Harlin gave her the finger and went into his apartment, where Martin Pugliese and a guy named Leo Scaglione were in his living room.

"Look who's our drummer," Martin said. Leo had narrow eyes and chocolate-colored skin, and Harlin remembered him from junior high, where Leo'd run a small business selling whip-its at age thirteen. Harlin nodded.

"Hey, Harlin," Martin said. "Guess where Leo's been."

"No idea," Harlin said, picking up the remote for the TV.

"Rehab," Leo said. "And you know what I did as soon as I got out?" He put down his drums and began rolling a joint.

"I went straight to a bar."

Martin raised his beer can and stretched his weird lady legs out in front of him as if it were he, not Harlin, who paid most of the rent.

"Twelve hundred dollars a week of state-mandated money, six weeks, and I walked out of there, walked into a bar, and drank three pitchers of Utica Club."

"And you're happy about that?" said Harlin.

Leo inhaled. "Yeah, I'm happy," he said.

"Here's to state-mandated rehab," Martin said.

"Now I drink a shot of whiskey every morning, just to wake myself up," Leo said.

"I smoke a bowl," said Martin.

"And you're happy," Harlin said.

Leo put down his drums and looked at Martin.

"You're happy, right, Leo?" Harlin said, a little louder.

"Yeah, I'm happy," Leo said. "Are you happy?"

Harlin stared at the two of them, their bloodshot eyes and haggard faces, and thought about the possibility of anyone ever letting them play music in public.

"No, I'm not happy," he said and went up to his room.

Now there were three of them, banging around downstairs, and Harlin found himself, tired, angry, and sad, sitting back on the same stool at Lucy's Tavern most nights of the week.

He saw Grace a few times after that and tried to pretend he didn't. She'd come in with Jimmy, who didn't say much to anyone, just sat there and stared at the television while Grace chatted with Rita and Benny Jackson. Then, when he was ready to go, he'd get Grace her coat and lead her out of the bar.

Winter went on in its own slow way. The sky grew more and more relentlessly gray, and people began to fight with each other. Next door, Fat Betty and her boyfriend replaced their boisterous sex with louder fights. Cyrus forgot to pay the electric bill, and Martin got kicked out of Lucy's for pulling a knife on the bouncer. Harlin got into a fight at Lucy's with Bill Kane about which produced more homosexuals, jail or military school, and that ended badly.

Then one night in the early spring, Harlin's luck changed. It was a balmy night, unseasonably warm, and as he came home from Lucy's, Harlin saw Grace standing on his front lawn. Why she turned up that night was a mystery he'd never solve. It just happened, the way things sometimes happened to Harlin, like the time he got arrested for walking into his first ex-wife's house and taking all the CDs, TV, and stereo equipment he had bought in the first place. But there she was, waiting as calmly and patiently as if she were waiting for a bus.

"I'm here for that drink you offered me," she said.

"You'd better come in then," said Harlin and led her up the back stairs, which went straight to the second floor and avoided his roommates in the living room downstairs.

Harlin and Grace started having sex the minute they got in the door. They did it standing up, sitting down, sideways, and in the filthiest positions Harlin could imagine. They drank half a bottle of whiskey in the process, and then they tried to do it again. Finally, they wore themselves out and just lay there.

"Damn, Harlin," said Grace. "Look at us."

"We look great," Harlin said. He passed her the bottle of whiskey, and she took some then passed it back to him.

Harlin put the bottle down on the floor by the mattress and ran a hand along the length of her. His fingers paused near a bruise on her rib cage. He had noticed it before, and now he took a good look and saw that it was substantial.

Grace caught him staring. "You should see what I did to the other guy," she said.

"Anyone can see what you did to him," Harlin said. "You married him."

Grace swallowed some whiskey.

"Harlin," she sighed. She took out a cigarette and lit a match. "Honey, you worry too much."

Harlin thought about reminding her that he didn't worry too much at all. In fact, she had pointed this out to him many times. A man who worried too much probably wouldn't smoke pot during his work breaks. A man who worried too much wouldn't keep driving drunk after his first arrest. Instead, he said, "You shouldn't let him do that to you."

"Don't lecture me," Grace said. "It's boring." She turned to face him, and as she did, one of her breasts fell onto his chest. She looked down at it.

"Remember how pretty they used to be?" she said. "Men used to come, just from looking at them." She let her breast go, and it moved off to the side beneath her armpit. "Anyway," she said. "Now I have to try a little harder."

Grace rolled over, her back to him, and pulled the sheet up around her. Harlin waited for her to talk some more, but instead he just heard her breathing slow.

She twitched a few times, and he knew that soon she'd be passed out, the way he should be by now. Harlin lit a cigarette and looked at her breasts, which, while looser than they used to be, were still in decent shape. Grace began to snore. He finished the bottle of whiskey and put his hand on her belly, which was soft and warm.

He knew that they had no business being in bed together and that he couldn't do anything to change or protect her. But still, as he felt her slipping away from him into sleep, he wanted something more, some assurance that what they'd once had still mattered.

"Grace," he whispered, nudging her a little. "Hey."

"Jimmy," she said. "Just let me sleep."

At first Harlin thought that was funny and laughed, but then when he heard his own laughter, alone in the room, it wasn't funny at all. He extricated himself from Grace, who didn't seem to notice his body's retreat. She lay there, sprawled out, lips parted, one arm flung across the pillow where he'd been.

Harlin put on a bathrobe and slippers, fumbled around for his cigarettes and lighter. Then he went downstairs for a drink. The music had stopped, and the place smelled like spilled beer and pot smoke. Martin and Cyrus were sitting at the kitchen table, smoking a joint and playing cards.

"Well, look who's here," Cyrus said. Harlin stepped over Martin's legs to get to the refrigerator. "What's up, little brother?"

"Is that my weed?" Harlin said.

"Did you have a woman up there tonight?" asked Martin.

"Answer my question," said Harlin.

"I think he did," Martin said. "I'm pretty sure I heard a woman up there."

"Who was it?" said Cyrus. "That know-it-all Linda Hartley?"

Harlin took the joint out of Cyrus's hand and breathed in.

"Who was it, Harlin?" Martin said. "Madeline Harris?"

Cyrus squinted at his little brother. "Grace?" he said.

Harlin said nothing.

"It was Grace," Cyrus said. "Grace Meyers. Man, Harlin, are you stupid."

Harlin didn't count to ten. He punched Cyrus in the jaw. Cyrus punched him back, but Harlin dodged it and his fist landed on Harlin's shoulder. They stood there breathing hard, staring at each other. Cyrus rubbed his jaw, and Harlin adjusted his bathrobe.

"I'm going out," Harlin said and slammed the door behind him.

It was a warm, still night with wisps of clouds pale against the moon. Harlin followed his own shadow around the block, rubbing his shoulder, waiting for his anger to fade. He kept walking until he got to Lucy's. The bar was closed, and Harlin put his head against the glass of the window and looked at the empty tables and chairs. After a while, he imagined he saw shapes in the gloom in front of him. He saw Grace laughing with Rita while Jimmy stared at the television. He saw Bill Kane propped up against the jukebox, drunk and grinning without showing any teeth. He saw Martin Pugliese lying to Rita about how much money he had, and in the corner by the bathroom he saw himself, slumped over a drink, watching the smoke from his cigarette make its way to the ceiling. He stood there a long time, imagining himself sitting there, day after day, a beer in his hands, drinking and not fighting, or drinking and fighting, while at home his brother's band played on, and on, and on.

It was beginning to get light when Harlin finally made his way home, taking the back route so that no one would see him wandering around still drunk in his bathrobe. As he approached the little patch of mud in front of Fat Betty's house, he saw three cats sitting in a tree staring down at him like monkeys. The cats watched him pass, and Harlin imagined that they were his ex-wives and girlfriends. He could practically hear them talking. *There he goes, slinking home in his bathrobe and slippers. That stupid man,* he imagined them saying, *when will he ever learn?*

Harlin lifted his shoulders and smiled. "Who knows, ladies?" he said to them all. "Who knows?" He forgave Grace then for saying her husband's name when she was in bed with him. After all, he often thought about other women in bed. All of them, really. He thought about her showing up just like that and wondered what had happened, if Jimmy had gotten too violent, or she could sense that he was going to, or whether she had just gotten restless, the way she often did with her men. He wondered if she would still be there sleeping when he got home. He hoped she was. He hoped she was still in his bed, so he could slip in beside her and bury his nose in the back of her neck, the way he had so many times before, when they'd been living together and then married and then the many times they'd fallen into bed together after they divorced. But he guessed she probably wasn't, and this reminded him of something his mother had said to his father after he'd insulted his boss and gotten himself fired from the salt mines, a good-paying job with benefits. "It's not disappointment that gets me with you," she'd said. "It's the hope."

Harlin kept walking toward his apartment full of his brother, an asshole who barely paid the rent, and the empty place in his bed left by the ex-wife he swore he'd never see again. But when he opened the door, Grace was still there. Naked in the dirty sheets, smelling like sour bourbon and cigarettes. She stirred when he slipped in beside her.

"Harlin," she said. "Where did you go?"

"Shhh," he said. "Go back to sleep."

Perhaps they both knew that it was the last time they would be together like this, that Grace would leave and they would both move on and later they might see each other in passing, or hear each other's news, but they wouldn't feel the heat of each other's skin, or the roughness of each other's hearts the way they did then. So they lay there for a while, falling in and out of sleep, wrapped around each other in the private, lavender time between night and day when anything can happen and sometimes, at least for a little while, all is forgiven.

NOT MUCH IS NEW HERE

On Thursday, a week before her neighbor was going to get married, Linda Hartley was sitting at her desk working on her latest column, which was called "Should You Tell?" In it was a letter from a reader who had kissed another man shortly after telling her boyfriend that she was in love with him.

"Should I tell him I kissed the other guy?" the reader had written. "Or should I just let it go, since I know I'm not going to do it again. I mean, what he doesn't know won't hurt him, right? Or me, right? I really am in love with my boyfriend. Please help. Luv, Dumbstruck."

Linda told Dumbstruck (who she had referred to as "Dear Reader") that honesty, in this case, depended on the relationship. "If you aren't going to marry him and don't see this going on forever, then you might not have to tell him," she wrote. "But the trouble with not telling him is that every lie you tell, even by omission, adds a layer of distance between the two of you. And by not telling him, you think you're protecting him, when really you're protecting yourself, which you'll discover when he eventually finds out the truth. People usually do, and that's how husbands/wives get shot, etc., etc."

Linda liked her answer, but then shortly after she turned the piece in, her new boyfriend, a nature journalist she'd met on a press trip to Hawaii, told her he had kissed another woman at a party.

"Actually, she kissed me," he said.

"For how long?" Linda said.

"It couldn't have been more than three or four seconds," he said. "And then I told her I had a girlfriend."

"One-one-thousand, two-one-thousand, three-one-thousand," Linda counted. "That's a pretty long time."

"Are you upset?" David said. "Seriously? I'm only telling you because I didn't want us to have any secrets. It meant nothing."

Ha, Linda thought. She remembered plenty of

kisses she'd had that meant nothing. They'd all been very hot and there was usually some groping involved, which was the last thing she wanted to imagine David, who didn't drink too much and understood wildflowers, doing with someone else at a party she wasn't invited to.

"I'm not upset," Linda said.

"Good," David said, and then he went off to the mountains to do a story on old-growth forests.

But she was upset, Linda thought now. She knew she shouldn't be. It was a long-distance relationship, and these things were to be expected. In fact, she may have even kissed another man if not twoish around the same time.

"But I didn't go telling everyone about it," she said to her cat, Walter. "No, sir. I kept my lying cakehole shut because it was no big deal and I didn't see the point of blabbing." The cat bit his own tail and then sat down on the obituary section of the newspaper.

Linda scratched him behind the ears. And worse, she thought, she normally wouldn't have cared. A three-second kiss at a party really didn't mean anything, as she of all people should know. But who knew if it was only three seconds? And she had fallen hard for David, whose gentle voice and sweet hands had made her feel safe the moment she'd met him. She'd spent three weeks with him, exploring the wild, unforgiving northern coastline of Hawaii, listening to him talk about lichens and moss (lichens and moss!—fascinating, it turned out) and generally having a very good time not writing her column. Since she'd come home, she'd been writing to him almost daily, and when she imagined his face touching this other woman's and his hands in her hair, she felt like throwing up.

"Should you tell?" she said, looking at her column. "No. Absolutely not. Unless you have herpes," she added. "Then maybe you should say something."

Outside she could hear her downstairs neighbor Dixie arguing with her fiancé, Paul, a giant cop with a face as muscled as a racehorse, about their upcoming wedding.

"In our driveway?" Paul was yelling. "The driveway? You're insane. You need medication. You need Ripatrim."

Linda didn't know what Ripatrim was, but it sounded like a combination of Dexatrim and Ritalin, both of which were basically speed and would make her neighbor a hundred times stronger than she already was.

Linda's neighbor Dixie was a Polish woman in her early forties. Her real name was something like Annika, but she had changed it to Dixie when she came to the States with her fiancé, who she met when he was in the army. "Dixie is much better," she said once to Linda. "Dixie is classy."

She was tall and fair with piles of wavy blond hair and a youthful face, which she kept firm by smearing an oatmeal and egg mask on it twice a week. Linda knew this because she had more than once come across Dixie in the garden or out on the front porch wearing hot pants, high heels, and a shower cap, her face a bright sunshine yellow.

"You should try this," she'd said to Linda. "Oatmeal and two eggs, twice in a week. No ugly lines." She'd pointed to the area between Linda's mouth and nose. Linda had thought about trying it (who wanted ugly line?), but the image of the two of them rattling around that giant, drafty house with breakfast on their faces was a little more than she could bear.

Now she heard Dixie yelling back at the person who had agreed to marry her.

"Hey!" she was yelling. "Why you bought this dumb-ass thing?"

Linda had no idea what they were talking about

but imagined the fight could go on all morning. She closed her window and sat down at her desk to work on a column but instead began a letter to her boyfriend.

"Dear David," she wrote.

It's mid-afternoon here, which makes it early morning there, and you are probably out worrying about invasive species, but thought I would write. I am sitting in my apartment looking out the window across the valley. It's so beautiful here right now. I know you're lucky to have gorgeous weather all year round, but the dreadful, gray winters here make June feel like a gift. From my balcony I can see the trees fade, from bright green to darker green to the blue, blue hills across the lake. It's different from the vibrant lushness that surrounds you in Hawaii—this is a gentler, softer beauty that sprawls for miles. I look at those hills and all that color fills my heart, even after growing up here. My friend Harlin—that guy from the bar I told you about who managed to get pepper-sprayed and sent to jail without leaving his own house—says he looks at all that color and all he sees is a hazy day. But to me, even the ditches look regal, full of daisies and baby cat-tails.

Anyway, not much is new here. My down-stairs door neighbor is engaged and is out in the front yard fighting with her fiancé, a giant cop named Paul, who she fights with con-stantly. I don't know what the problem was today, although it probably has something to do with Dixie suspecting Paul of lying to her. (She thinks all men are liars. And no offense, but she might be right, frankly.) Last week she got mad at him for not telling her that he'd used her business line to call his mother. She was out in the yard screaming at him for a good fifteen minutes until finally he stopped and turned around and said, "Woman! Settle down, or I will call the police." I thought this was hilarious since he is the police, and all that meant was that he was going to call his friend Dale and go get a beer, but it shut Dixie up, which is hard to do, and he turned neatly on his heel and strode off to his cruiser. Two minutes later I saw Dixie out in her garden as if nothing had happened, waiting for someone

to come along so she could show them her
ring, which she's been doing happily ever since
she got engaged.

Linda stopped writing for a minute and read what she'd written. Blah, blah, blah. Everything is fine. She picked up her pencil and started writing again.

Oh, David. I want to write you a long,
funny letter about my life here, but the truth is
my heart isn't in it. I'm still upset about you
and that other woman at the party. I know I
shouldn't care. I mean, so you kissed another
woman. Big deal. I showed Harlin Wilder my
push-up bra last night at the bar and didn't
think twice about it. (Although admittedly
that was just looking, not touching, and the
bra really is fantastic. You should see it. My
tits are up to my shoulders!) But I do care. I
wish you were here, and that I was the woman
you were kissing at parties. Or anywhere else,
really.

Anyway, I guess that's all really, except that I
miss you. I can't believe it will be another
month until we see each other again, and I get

*to fall asleep after you've kissed the back of my
shoulder good night. I wish it was sooner.*

Love,
Linda

Linda looked over her last paragraph and crossed it
out. Then she put the letter in a folder labeled "Letters Not Sent." And since there was no one there to
kiss the back of her shoulder or anywhere else, she
put on some lipstick and a pair of nice heels and
went out to the bar.

At Lucy's, Stewart Levine and Harlin Wilder were
sitting next to the jukebox having a conversation
about the trip Harlin was about to take with his new
girlfriend. The drive, Harlin said, was going to be full
of activities.

"She's got a log-in list in the glove compartment
where she wants me to log in all this crap—land-
marks, state troopers, 'Oh, there's that kind of bird
here.'" He shook his head. "I'm not doing it."

"Good for you," said Stewart.

"For one thing," said Harlin, "I can't read and
write while the car's moving because I get sick. And
for another thing, I don't want to."

"If you do what she tells you to do, the next

thing you know, your balls are in her purse," said Stewart.

"Her old man is even worse," said Harlin. "He's an engineer, and he has a formula for everything: eating, dressing, driving—he even has a formula for watching TV. Sometimes he's in there watching *I Love Lucy*, and he hates Lucy, but it all has to do with the color he's wearing and how many days are left until his birthday."

They cleared a spot for Linda, who sat down between them and ordered a vodka tonic. "Well," she said, "we all have problems."

Harlin nodded. "My girlfriend is bossy and her father's insane and I have to drive twenty hours just to spend time with the two of them," he said.

"I hate my mother and I live with her," said Stewart.

"My new boyfriend kissed another girl," said Linda. They clinked their glasses and drank. "Actually," Linda said, "he says she kissed him and then he told her he had a girlfriend."

"If he told you he kissed her, he must have done a lot more than that," said Harlin.

"Oh, come on," Linda said. "You think so?"

"Sure. That's guilt talking, and who feels guilty about a three-second kiss?" said Harlin.

"Not you, obviously," said Linda. Or him, she thought as her ex-boyfriend Austin sauntered over and sat down next to Stewart. Speaking of untrustworthy men, Linda thought, pretending not to notice him. She hadn't seen much of Austin since they'd broken up for good, because she'd been careful to go to the bar on nights that she knew he was working late in the fields, or driving a truck for the salt mines, which he did in the cold months when work eased up on the farm. Now, being near him made her uncomfortable, so she didn't look him in the eye.

"Did I interrupt something?" said Austin, ordering a beer.

"Linda's new boyfriend kissed another woman," said Harlin.

Linda kicked him, and Harlin looked at her as if to say, "What did I do?"

"He must have done a lot more than that if he told you about it," said Austin.

"You're the expert," Linda said.

"Actually, I believe that's your line of work," Austin said.

"Touché," said Linda, annoyed that Austin was smart.

"Well, at least he did tell you," Stewart said.

"Yes," added Harlin. "You have to give the guy credit for that. You have to like a woman to want to be that honest."

"*Like* me?" Linda said. "I think he hates me. What kind of a jackass kisses another woman and then *tells* you about it, three minutes after you've said you feel lucky you met him?"

"A guilty jackass," said Harlin.

"Guilty, guilty, guilty," said Austin.

"You should go out with my friend Roscoe," said Stewart. "That man is a prize. He let this nineteen-year-old beautiful Irish girl crash at his house, and he treated her like gold. Didn't even touch her. Not that abstaining makes him exceptional. Oh wait, yes it does. Delete that."

"Delete, delete, delete," said Harlin.

"Well, you don't want girls taking advantage of you," Austin said. He reached into his T-shirt for his wallet, and Linda looked at his hands, which were smudged with grease. He must have been working on his car, which meant he was trying to cut back on his drinking again. When they had been together, he used to work on a 1967 Valiant he'd bought to stay out of the bar and she used to go to the garage and keep him company. She remembered how much she had liked sipping coffee and reading the paper while he dismantled the fan belt or coaxed the engine. It had been so nice to sit in the sun and watch him work and know that for a while everything was fine, that they were a normal couple who could eat breakfast together or read the newspaper. But he never read the newspaper, she reminded herself. And she never ate breakfast.

"What if he's telling the truth and she kissed him?" Linda said. "He did tell her he had a girlfriend—that's more than most men would do."

"Maybe," said Stewart.

"Doubtful," said Austin. He excused himself and went to the bathroom to wash up and change his shirt.

Stewart and Harlin looked at the television. Linda drank some more and missed the way she'd been when she hadn't been in love with anyone. She'd felt so brave then, like anything could happen.

"You know," she said out loud to no one. "I think I was happiest when I didn't have any boyfriend at all. No one tells you that. No one tells women how much better it is to be single than attached to someone."

"You should put that in one of your columns," said Harlin.

"Nah," Linda said. "I never put what I really think

in my columns. Procter and Gamble would pull all their ads." Or worse, she guessed, her readers might stop reading what she wrote. And then what would happen to her? Without her readers, sometimes she wondered if she would even exist.

"You can't just keep romping around with strangers, though," Harlin said. "One of these days you're going to have to settle down."

"Do we want to give advice out like that, here at the bar?" said Stewart. "I don't think that's a good idea. I think as a longtime regular and walking relationship disaster, it is your job to keep shit like that under your hat."

Austin came out of the bathroom wearing a vintage cowboy shirt. His looks were made for a bar, Linda thought. An angular face with strong bones that caught the overhead lights, auburn hair that he wore in a crew cut all summer but that grew into a rust-colored thicket in the winter and fall. Linda watched him playing pool, seeing him by turns as an ordinary boy in a cowboy shirt he'd found at the Salvation Army and then as the taut-bellied man to whom she would have given the moon.

"Do you think it's possible to meet the right person and then completely screw it up?" Linda said.

"How is it not possible?" said Harlin. "Most people aren't with the person they're supposed to be with."

Across the room, Austin was flirting with a school teacher named Elizabeth and two of her friends. He started to dance with one of them—Rebecca or Rachael, or whatever her name was, Linda couldn't remember. She didn't like seeing his hands on the small of the other woman's back, and the fact that she didn't made her a little sick of herself. Oh, whatever, she told herself. Let Austin be someone else's problem. Let someone else soothe his drunk, lonely soul.

"Do you think you missed your true love?" Linda asked Harlin.

"There's a question," said Harlin. "That's like when that woman Sarah, no her name was Deborah, asked me if I still loved my last wife."

"I asked you that once and you ran to the bathroom," Linda said, a little annoyed, since she liked to think of herself as the woman at the bar who asked the most provocative questions. Was Elizabeth wearing one of Austin's shirts?

"Listen, given that I once loved my last wife enough to marry her, you'd hope I wouldn't hate her,"

Harlin said. "And given that kind of a nosy question, going to the bathroom is a pretty good response."

The next morning Linda was working on a new column about how not to backstab other girls ("Beats me," she wrote later to David. "I've been backstabbing other girls my whole life. But I do that to men, too, so at least I'm not sexist about it") when Dixie came upstairs.

"Oh, Linda," she said, walking in and sitting down on Linda's daybed. "I don't know if I can go through with wedding."

Linda glanced at her unfinished column. She was on deadline and didn't quite have time to talk to Dixie about her fiancé. But she had a soft spot for her neighbor, who wore her heart on her sleeve and whose sentences, with little time for prepositions or articles, went straight for the jugular. Also, the last time she'd told Dixie she couldn't talk because she'd had to work, Dixie had said, "Ha ha. You don't work. You sit around all day talking on telephone drinking too much coffee," and pulled up a chair anyway.

"Tell me what happened," Linda said.

"Stomach is all bad," Dixie said now. "Back of my head is all wrong. Something is stuck there, won't go away."

She picked up a copy of *Sugar and Spice*, one of the magazines Linda wrote for, and then set it down again.

"Want to know funny thing?" she said. "The other night I have dream, only time father come to me in dream since he died. He say me, do not marry him, and nod to a man."

"Was the man Paul?" Linda asked.

"I don't know," Dixie said. "Couldn't see face. But after dream, back of my head not right. Something is stuck. First time he come to me in dream. Even after he died, I am crying. I am asking him, begging for him to please come back, nothing. Now, twenty years later, I am about to have first wedding—and now he comes to me in dream."

Outside Linda could hear Paul gently talking to the lawn mower.

"Maybe your father is trying to let you go," she said. "Maybe he wants you to be happy."

"Happy?" Dixie said. "Who says marriage is about being happy? More like promise. You write for magazine, you should know."

Linda sighed. "I never said I knew everything," she said.

Dixie smiled at her, almost tenderly. "I know," she said. "Just act that way sometimes."

Later, at the bar, Linda sat with Harlin, who had just gotten off work and was avoiding going back to his own apartment.

"There's trouble in paradise," Linda said. "My neighbor's having second thoughts about her marriage."

Harlin took out his wallet and carefully counted out the money he had. Linda shoved her own money toward Rita, to indicate that the next round was on her.

"Paul's not a bad man, and Dixie's not an easy woman," Harlin said. He knew Paul from his own interactions with the police, and he knew Dixie from some conversations about Paul she'd had with him while waiting in line at the bank. You wouldn't know it to look at him, but Harlin was a very good listener. And like Linda Hartley, he tended to enjoy other people's business as much as his own. "She could do a lot worse."

Linda took one of Harlin's cigarettes, which she knew irritated him, especially since she didn't really smoke. She knew she wasn't fooling anyone, but she felt glamorous when she faked her way through a cigarette. I am sexy, she'd think, holding the smoke in her mouth for a few seconds and then exhaling it slowly. I am very hot. Austin was playing pool with Stewart Levine, and Linda caught him staring at her. She looked back at him and then quickly away as Harlin offered her a light, a look that did not go unnoticed by Harlin.

"He adored you, you know," he said. He put his pack of cigarettes back in his shirt pocket, out of her reach. "I could never get out of him what happened. You two broke up all the time, and I could never get him to tell me what finally put the nail in the coffin."

Linda thought about that for a minute. There were so many things that had killed her relationship with Austin. The way he didn't come home when he said he would, how hard it was for them to fit into each other's worlds outside the bar, the way they clawed at each other's soft spots until they'd forgotten what they'd liked about each other in the first place.

"He drank too much," she said.

"Uh-huh," Harlin said.

"And once, he called me another woman's name in bed," Linda added. "How tacky is that? I mean, if someone is nice enough to let you into her house and take off her clothes, you should remember her name."

"It *is* good manners," Harlin admitted.

"He called me Brenda," Linda said, nodding at Brenda, who was playing darts at the other end of the bar. "Then when I kicked him out, he said I shouldn't be mad because he was only joking and Brenda wouldn't want to go out with him anyway because she's married."

Over by the pool table, Stewart Levine was heckling Austin. "When was the last time you bought a new shirt?" he said.

"The thing is," Harlin said, "he can't help it. The guy gets depressed, and instead of feeling sad or moping around, he goes out and does something dumb to himself. My old man was like that. He was a nice man, but he drank himself to death by the time he was forty-nine. The drinking had him. And even though he loved my mother, *loved* her, she had to leave him."

"Just like I had to leave Austin," Linda said sadly.

"Seriously," said Stewart. "That shirt looks like it's

about thirty years old, and it stinks like the cowboy who used to own it is still in it."

"Yeah," Harlin said. "But Austin did love you. He really did."

"Oh, who knows who loves anyone?" Linda said later to her cat, after she'd tottered back to her drafty house. And so what if Austin loved her? She had loved him, too, but it was too much work to love a man like that. David was much better.

"Relationships take work, but they shouldn't violate labor laws," she said to the cat and then pulled out a Post-it and wrote that down.

She checked her machine, which contained no message from David, and went into her kitchen, where her crisper was on the floor. In its place in the refrigerator was a six-pack of Beck's beer that did not belong to Linda. Linda sighed. After her neighbor had come up to tell her about her dream, she'd asked if she could store her champagne in her refrigerator before the wedding, Linda had said yes, and since then the woman had been in and out of the apartment as if Linda had given her carte blanche. First a pair of scissors Linda had never seen before turned up on her stove, then the copy of *Town & Country* "Weddings" had appeared on the living room table, and once Dixie herself was in the living room, weaving together a practice bouquet of lilies.

"Got lilies for cheap," she'd said.

"Dixie," Linda had said. "How did you get in here?"

"Funny thing," Dixie had said. "My key works in your lock." Linda sighed. "You can't be in here when I'm not here."

Dixie had looked her up and down, as if seeing her for the first time. "You lost weight?" she'd said.

"No."

"Huh," Dixie had said. "I think so. Chin is all gone."

Linda shoved her crisper aside and took out one of Dixie's beers. How had she gotten herself into this? First David had put information in her head she didn't want there, and now Dixie was putting all this stuff in her apartment, and Harlin was making her feel bad about leaving her ex-boyfriend, which had been the smartest thing she'd done in a long time. And why hadn't David called? If he liked her so much, why hadn't he picked up the phone? So what if he was in the backwoods of Hawaii? There were pay phones in Hawaii. There were phone cards. He was probably off messing around with a botanist who could hula and play the ukulele. "I think I would be much prettier if I could hula and play the ukulele," she said to her cat.

There was a tap, a light smattering sound on her window, and Linda looked outside to see her ex-boyfriend Austin on the front lawn of the apartment house, throwing pennies up at the glass. She opened the window.

"Stop it," she said, a little uneasy at how pleased she was to see him. "You'll wake up Dixie."

"Then let me in," he said.

"I'll come down."

Austin was drunk, of course, but so was Linda, so that worked out okay. They sat on the front porch listening to the creek that ran through town. Earlier in the evening there had been a thundershower, and the air, lush and warm, hinted of wild sweet peas and phlox. Austin put his hand on Linda's leg. "You smell good," he said.

After sitting at the bar for three hours in the heat, sweating, sipping vodka, and pretending to smoke,

Linda thought she probably smelled like Keith Richards. Still, it was a nice thing for him to say, and she leaned into him.

"I'm in love with someone else now, you know," she said.

"I know," Austin said. "I'll find someone else, too, one of these days." He didn't say it in an antagonistic way, more like it was just a fact they both knew, and Linda fought a pang of jealousy, then sadness. Of course he would find someone else. He would find another broken woman at Lucy's, make her feel beautiful and adored, and then, when she was back on her feet again, he'd start drinking too much and fooling around and generally giving her excuses to leave him until she would. But while they were together, their affair would be like something in the movies, and she'd leave him feeling like she'd gotten to know sides of herself she'd forgotten existed. That was the way it was, Linda thought. Austin's women always thought they were fixing him, although really it was the other way around.

"Does he make curfew?" Austin said.

"Ha, ha," Linda said. "Yes. Not that it's any of your business."

Austin nodded. He didn't like to draw out conversations like this one, Linda knew. This is it, she thought. We'll say goodbye now, and then the next time we see each other all we'll do is make small talk. She tried to think of a clever way to say good-bye first, some way to honor what they'd had without getting too maudlin. But Austin spoke before she did.

"I need to know something," he said. "Was it all my fault?"

The frankness of his question surprised her, and Linda thought about telling him, yes, it was his fault—he had stopped coming home when he said he would and he'd called her Brenda in bed and he'd flirted shamelessly with Elizabeth Teeter. But she knew that was only half the truth. It was her fault, too. She'd slept with other people and acted like his drinking was the only thing keeping them apart. Mostly, though, she had needed him to love her more than she loved him.

"It wasn't *all* your fault," she said.

She thought Austin would leave then, but he didn't. Instead he put his head down, his hands around the back of his neck. "I didn't want to fuck this one up," he said, and Linda thought he might cry.

She tried to think of all the things she could say, like of course he did on some level; if he didn't, he might have come home before 3:00 A.M. on her birthday. She thought of all the things he'd done and how much easier, how much more right it was to be with someone like David. But then she looked at Austin, and all she could think about was how beautiful he was and how much chemistry they'd had. She knew what would happen if she went back to him. She could see the other women flitting about in his peripheral vision, the drunken rampage that would resurface in the fall, when the days grew shorter and he didn't spend as much time in the fields. This was what had always plagued her after his breathing deepened and his head rested on her belly and she lay awake in the dark. Still, it was so hard to let him go. We really had something, she wanted to say. Sometimes when we were together, it was magic.

Austin ran his hand over his hair, which was close-cropped to his skull for summer. Linda put her arm around his waist and pressed her face into his shoulder, and when he began to kiss her, she couldn't see saying goodbye any other way, so she kissed him back. And when they went upstairs and he began to take off her clothes, she took off his, and when, in the morning, she heard him leave, she felt the whole thing turn into her own secret, one that she would keep for a while, close to her heart.

It was early afternoon the next day when Dixie called, wanting to know if Linda could go pick up her wedding dress. "I don't want new husband to see," she said. "It's bad luck."

"I'm a little busy today," Linda said.

"Funny thing," Dixie said. "This morning I think I see your ex-boyfriend leave apartment."

"Really?" Linda said. "How strange."

"Not my business," Dixie said, "but I say to Paul, What he is doing here? I hope he is not with Linda. Bad, bad thing, if she go back to him. No one wants that. New boyfriend sounds much better."

"I'll pick up your dress around three," Linda said.

"Then again," Dixie said, "not a bad way to get back at new boyfriend for kissing another woman."

That night a fight crept up through the heating vent and Linda heard Dixie crying. The next morning, when she went out to get coffee, she saw Paul bundled up in a sleeping bag, asleep in his cruiser in front of the house.

A few days later, the day of her neighbor's wedding, Linda was at her desk, composing another letter to David. It had been cold and rainy for a week, and everyone, including her, was in a soggy mood.

"Dear David," she wrote.

> *I know what you mean about having a complicated relationship with being alone. Last night I had the whole night to myself in my apartment just to read and put things away and listen to Johnny Cash. (Do you like Johnny Cash? My mother hates him. She's a retired psychiatric nurse and says that that's what all the men in her unit used to listen to. They would beat up their wives or go out and get into some racist fight, and then they'd get suicidal, come onto her unit, and sit around crying and listening to Johnny Cash and feeling sorry for themselves. I told her I'm not suicidal and can't even throw a good punch, but she says it's depressing, listening to those yahoos plink away on*

*their guitars and carry on about women they
lost because they were too stupid to act like
men. Still, I love Johnny Cash and totally iden-
tify with his songs.)*

*Anyway, I kept thinking, Oh, thank God, a
night to myself. No drink dates or lunch dates or
any other obligations. But you should have
heard me in March, when I had a few weeks of
nights to myself. I was a nightmare.*

*Oh, David, your last letter sounded distant
and a little businesslike, which makes me feel
foolish, sending you long, newsy letters that take
me days to write. Aren't you a little madly in
love with me? It would be so convenient if you
were.*

Linda stopped and drew a line through that last paragraph. Ugh, she thought. I'll just chase him away. She
started again.

*Not much is new here. Last night I went out
to my bar and had a lovely time. It's such a
comfort to be a regular at a bar, especially when
you live alone. I mean that in the least pathetic,
nicest possible way. I saw almost everyone I*

wanted to see and got caught up on some of the
gossip. Hank and Sarah, who run the restau-
rant next door, have finished their new house,
and Rita, the lesbian bartender who sometimes
has sex with men, is through with her girl-
friend. I have never met her girlfriend, but Rita
assures me that she's brilliant, and has perfect,
perfect breasts. Unfortunately, she had been
sharing some of that perfection with a graduate
student named Anka, and naturally Rita is a lit-
tle upset.

Anyway, it was well into happy hour, and
everyone was drunk. Hank Stevens (the cook I
told you about with the metal plate in his head)
was wearing the shrieking red and yellow shirt
I got him in Hawaii, and Austin Jones, who I
used to go out with, did an impromptu hula
demonstration to Jimmy Buffett's "Margari-
taville." Harlin Wilder made a pretty good at-
tempt at playing a ukulele that's been hanging
on the wall by the piano for about thirty years,
and everybody bought everyone else drinks. I
sat there remembering what it is that I love
about a small-town bar, the way it's like a per-
fect family, always there if you need it, but if

you need to leave it for a while and get away,
you can.

There was a knock at her door, and Dixie let herself into Linda's apartment. She was all made up, her yellow hair in a thick braid and piled on top of her head with honeysuckle blossoms woven into it. Linda slid her letter into her "Letters Not Yet Sent" file.

"Dixie," she said. "If you don't stop letting yourself into my apartment, I'm going to have to sue you."

"Time to get ready," said Dixie, tapping on her watch. Linda picked up the black dress she had laid out on her bed for the wedding. Dixie frowned.

"This is what you wear?" she said. "No, no. This is a wedding. Happy occasion. Wear something with color. Your country has foolish ideas about clothes." She walked into Linda's closet and pulled out a red satin skirt and blue satin top that didn't go together at all.

"Those don't really go together," Linda said.

"No, no, looks ravishing," Dixie said, and Linda put them on anyway. Oh well, she thought. It wasn't like they were leaving the house.

"Back of my head is still not good," Dixie said glumly while Linda got dressed. "Yesterday he is saying, Okay, we gotta try. Try? Marriage is life. What, he thinks it is like clothes? You can't try on a marriage!"

"Maybe you should call it off," Linda said. She felt bad as soon as she said it, but she was in a dark mood. She blamed it on the weather.

"Too late," said Dixie. "I never love any man like this one. Never."

She helped Linda with the zipper on the back of her satin shirt, and then Linda helped her pull on her wedding dress—an off-white satin tunic with elegant beading along the neckline. They both stopped talking when the dress was on to look at Dixie in the mirror. She was a lovely bride—tall and pale, her hair curling tenderly about her face. Linda fought a pang of jealousy. Oh, husband, husband, she thought, where can you be? If not David, then who?

"Look pretty good," said Dixie. She turned to examine her generous backside, then faced the mirror again. "Someday, Linda," she said. "This will be you."

"Maybe," Linda said.

"Oh, definitely," said Dixie. "You have a pretty heart, and strong head. Everything will be all right for you, don't worry."

To her surprise, Linda thought she might cry. She busied herself pulling the veil down over Dixie's face. Dixie must have felt emotional, too, because her veil trembled a little, and Linda offered her some vodka. But she couldn't bear the smell of it, so Linda drank the shot herself.

The wedding was in the backyard and was officiated by a judge named Bruce Lyman. Paul said "I do" before the judge finished the vows, but when it was Dixie's turn, she couldn't speak. She tried, but nothing came out. Paul put his hand on her hip to steady her.

"It's all right, sweetie," said the judge. "It will all be over soon."

Dixie's veil shook. She opened her mouth, but a raspy voice, not her own, came out. Finally she cleared her throat and repeated the vows. "I take you . . . all that is mine is now yours . . . ," but when it was time to promise to trust and cherish, she choked on the word *trust*.

"You can do it, Dixie," Judge Lyman said. "It won't hurt."

Linda got mad at him then, talking to her as if she were a child. It probably would hurt, Linda thought, but wasn't that the point? That marriage was a ridiculously hard thing to do? Here Dixie was, marrying Paul, and he loved her. And even though something was stuck in the back of Dixie's head, and her father's ghost was haunting her dreams, they were agreeing to take care of each other for life. For life! Against all odds, which was a miraculous and courageous thing to do. Like penguins, Linda thought. Monogamous, flightless birds who could swim. Unlikely. Flukes of nature. But somehow wonderful and full of grace.

The judge pronounced them man and wife, and when her new husband kissed her, Dixie blushed like a twenty-year-old. Then she hugged Linda, clinging to her like a barnacle.

After the wedding, they all had champagne, and then Linda went back upstairs to her apartment. She sat in her living room in her bright, shining outfit, looking at the old, high windows and shiny hardwood floors. She thought of something Dixie had told her when she first moved in. "House was built in eighteen forty-five. First is owned by sisters, then their daughters, now our landlady, Irene. Only women ever own this house." Linda wondered how many other women had stood in those rooms, fearful and nervous at the love in their hearts.

The cat jumped on her lap, and Linda thought that now would be a perfect time for her new boyfriend to call. "Ring," she said to the phone. The phone was still. "Ring," she said again. "What's the matter with you? It's the only job you have. *Ring!*"

But the phone was silent, and she felt a little sad, partly because it was gray and rainy outside, and perhaps because weddings often made her feel lonely. How did I get here? she thought. And where is the music?

Later, at the bar, she sat with Stewart Levine and Harlin Wilder. Stewart had just announced that he had fallen in love with a Mexican-American woman he met online, and he was driving west to go see her.

"Does she rock your world?" Harlin was saying.

"That's none of your business," Stewart said.

"Listen," Harlin said, "I've been married four times and divorced four times, and all I'm saying is that she'd better rock your world."

Linda told them about Dixie's wedding, and Stewart said good for Dixie. Now she and Paul wouldn't be wandering around by themselves like everyone else in the world.

"She choked on the word *trust*," Linda said.

"She should have," said Harlin. "No one in their right mind trusts the person they marry right away. You have to earn that shit."

"Why doesn't anyone ever tell you that?" said Stewart.

"Ask the advice columnist," said Harlin.

It was a good point, and Linda wrote it down on a cocktail napkin.

"Just be sure you quote me," Harlin said.

It was evening, and the bar was beginning to take on the cozy, womblike feel it always got after happy hour, when people had had just enough to drink to like themselves and forgive each other. Linda, on her second bourbon, started to feel as if she could understand all of the joy and sadness in the world, and it was kind of sweet, like a lullaby. She watched the other couples around her, Janet and Cyrus Wilder, twice married, twice divorced; Alice Lovejoy, still in love with her first husband, who died; and Benny Jackson, still in love with his ex-wife and maybe in

love with Alice. Over in the corner she saw Austin listening attentively to Elizabeth Teeter, whose husband,
the last Linda knew, was fooling around with a man.
She remembered what Harlin had said about Austin
really loving her. It isn't enough to love someone, she
thought. You have to live with them, too. She thought
about how eagerly Paul had said "I do," and hoped he
wasn't spending his wedding night in his cruiser.

Harlin and Stewart had started listing the number
of people they knew who cheated on each other right
before their weddings. Hank Stevens, Dale Hradisky.
Alice Lovejoy, who had made out with Randy, her
hairdresser, shortly after she said her vows.

It occurred to Linda that it might just be human
nature to mess up one more time when you met the
right person. That that was why her reader had
kissed someone else right after she decided she was
in love with her boyfriend, and it was probably why
David had kissed another girl at the party. And
maybe it was why she had had sex with Austin right
after she had fallen for someone else. Not that that
was anyone's business but her own. And anyway, that
was totally different.

From his seat next to her, Stewart proposed a
toast.

"To weddings," he said. "To me and my Arizona cupcake!"

"To weddings," Harlin and Linda agreed. They raised their glasses and made a toast, to Dixie's wedding and all weddings—as improbable as Linda's outfit and as common as the rain.

How to Save
a Wounded Bird

Two weeks after her husband, Bobby, left her for a man, Elizabeth Teeter's cat got into a bird's nest. At first she thought it was funny, Roger dangling from the neighbor's trellis like a giant black apostrophe, but then she saw the nest woven into the ivy at the top, and something small, blue-gray, and downy hanging from Roger's mouth.

"Goddammit, Roger!" she said and went across the lawn to get the bird from the cat's mouth. It was a baby, probably two weeks old, most of its skin still leathery, with a bulbous head too heavy for its neck. Elizabeth stared at it for a moment, thinking that all mothers have to love such ugly little things. She could see the mother bird sitting on a telephone wire, crying sharply. Roger ran under the porch and looked at her, his eyes like slits.

The baby bird seemed stunned but mostly unharmed, and Elizabeth decided to try to put it back in the nest. She was halfway up the neighbor's trellis when her neighbor, Allen, came home with his wretched dog, Otto.

Elizabeth waved.

"I have to put this bird back in its nest," she said.

Allen stood on tiptoe and peered at the bird. Elizabeth noticed his tan, which he kept year-round. Odd for upstate New York, she thought, especially if you were an accountant.

"Look, Otto," Allen said to his dog. "She has a bird."

Elizabeth sighed. She used to make fun of people for talking to their pets. Like her father, and the way he would talk to his dog—"Look, Stanley, Elizabeth is here. Isn't that great? Lizard is here for a visit!"—as if the dog were going to run upstairs and put clean sheets on the bed. But ever since her husband had gone, she'd been just as bad. "How did you sleep, Roger?" "Want some oatmeal for breakfast?"

"Can you reach the nest?" she said to her neighbor. "You're taller."

"The mother won't touch it after you have," Allen said. "They hate the smell of humans."

"Birds have little or no sense of smell," Elizabeth said, quoting a paper Trevor, one of her freshman students, had written about ducks.

Looking like he'd rather stick an ice pick in his eye, Allen took the bird and dumped it back in the nest. The mother bird still hadn't stopped crying.

"My cat got it," Elizabeth said, moving away from the nest so Allen would do the same and let the mother get back to her offspring.

"That's a fat cat," said Allen.

"Roger's not fat. He's big-boned," Elizabeth said. Allen's dog was sniffing around her lawn as if he was looking for a toilet.

"He looks like he could eat a house." Allen still hadn't moved away from the nest. "If you put a muzzle on that cat, he wouldn't eat the birds."

Elizabeth stared at his tight body, his muscled face, and wondered if he had ever kissed her husband. The thought made her tired. There was a time when she'd thought that being left for a man wouldn't be as bad as being left for a woman because she wouldn't feel as if it was her fault. But now even good-looking *men* made her feel bad about herself.

"If you put a diaper on your dog, he wouldn't shit in our yard," she said. "My yard," she added a second later, but Allen was already unlocking his door and letting himself into his house.

Elizabeth went back to her own porch, where Roger was lying down, licking the underside of his tail. She put him in the house, although she knew he'd start howling and pacing if she tried to keep him inside for more than a day. A ball of rage that had been burning in her throat, low and steady for days, flared. Goddamn Bobby, she thought, leaving her with this cat, these birds, four classes to teach, and no lover of her own. It was insensitive. He had terrible timing. He couldn't have picked a worse year to be gay.

The cat was beginning to pace and yowl, and Elizabeth guessed he'd only get worse if she kept him locked up, and he'd go straight back to the nest if she let him outside. She wondered if she should move the nest but then worried that that would make things worse. Finally she called the Wildlife Center downtown, where she got a machine and left a long message with all the details: rotten cat, antagonistic neighbor's porch, baby bird, should she move the nest? Then she heard herself say, "I'd like to resolve this conflict as peacefully as possible," as if she were the secretary of state.

Which was an alarming way for an aspiring Buddhist to feel. At the community college where Elizabeth taught, her classes were full of conservative students glowing with nationalism. They frightened her with their blind flag-waving, with how quickly they'd divided the world into good and evil. Once, when she'd questioned the validity of the Vietnam War, Trevor, the student who had written about ducks, left her a note saying she was creating an unpatriotic learning environment. "I thought this was a writing class," he'd written. "Not a hippie course on liberalism."

Hippie? she'd thought. *Hippie!* These shoes came from Barneys, young man.

The Wildlife Center didn't call back right away, and Elizabeth decided to feed the cat a hot dog, then let him out again, which seemed to work at least for the rest of the afternoon.

The next day, Elizabeth, still concerned about the birds next door, looked for some binoculars so she could sit on her own porch and keep an eye on the nest without having to deal with her neighbor. They weren't in the study or the "outdoor drawer" her husband had labeled in the kitchen, and after searching for close to an hour Elizabeth decided her husband must have taken them. Why? she thought. Why would he take the binoculars? She imagined him in a motel room somewhere using them to spy on other men. Don't be ridiculous, she thought. Just because he's attracted to men doesn't mean he's sitting in a motel somewhere peeping at one naked, you homophobe. But she couldn't stop feeling like his sex drive had suddenly become dark and seedy, like he was part of a wild, erotic club she couldn't get into. She envisioned him getting blow jobs in bathrooms, having group sex with beautiful men. It made her stomach hurt and was kind of a turn-on. She didn't know what was worse, the fact that he'd left her for a man, or that suddenly his sex life had become more exotic than hers.

Not that this was necessarily true. Both Elizabeth and Bobby had known what they were getting into when they married. Elizabeth knew he'd slept with a man in college, and he knew she'd had an affair with a woman. (Albeit brief, and mostly above the waist.) They were a modern couple, Elizabeth had thought. Renaissance thinkers. When her friend Madeline Harris had asked her if she worried he'd leave her for a man, she'd said, "He could just as easily leave me for a woman." But she hadn't wanted to be left at all, which was why she got married in the first place. And now he was gone and he'd taken the binoculars, her Kitty Wells CD, and six years of her life. She took some Atavan a friend had given her, and when that didn't work, she had some gin, too.

Elizabeth wound up on her porch standing on a chair looking at Allen's birds through a pair of mother-of-pearl opera glasses her grandmother had given her as a wedding present. When the phone rang, she hoped it was her husband, as this was precisely the kind of scene he'd love, like the time she'd fallen off her bicycle on her way home from a party because she was drunk and yelling, "Do you like my blue raincoat? It's new!" to the garbagemen. But then she let the machine pick up, because if it was Bobby, what would she say? Why now? I gave you so much time to figure this out before we got married. I could kill you for doing this to me. Please come home.

It was a man from the Wildlife Center, leaving a

message. He confirmed her student's information—birds will not abandon a baby once a human has touched it—but advised her not to move the nest. Elizabeth liked his deep, calm voice, his knowledge of small, wounded things. "All I can tell you is to try to control the cat," he said, adding, "If you give me a call back, I'd be happy to help you any way I can." Would you? she thought. Really? She almost wept then, but the moment passed.

The next Monday, right before she had to teach, Elizabeth saw her cat with a bird in his mouth again. This one had feathers and looked more like a real bird than the one he'd found the week before, and when she got it away from him, she saw that while there was some of Roger's saliva on its neck, there wasn't a deep bite. She called the Wildlife Center and got the same man who'd left a message on her machine. He told her to fill a bottle with hot water, wrap it in a towel, make a nest for the bird in a box, and bring it to the center.

"I have to teach a class," Elizabeth said.

"We're open until six. Bring the bird. If it's been in the cat's mouth, it's going to need antibiotics."

The bird was coming out of shock, its eyes bright and alert. It began to cry for food, or its mother— who knew? The cat was pacing outside, meowing. "Shut up, Roger," Elizabeth said. "Your instincts are horrible."

She put the bird in her bike basket and wobbled to school, a little worried that she'd give the bird, who was in total blackness in the box, a heart attack. "It's all right," she said. "Everything is going to be fine." It occurred to her that no one could see the bird, which made it look like she was riding her bike, reassuring herself, and the irony of that was not lost on her. By the time she got to the main office of the English department, the bird was rustling around. "We're going to check the mail," Elizabeth said, "and then we're going to class."

Her mailbox was full of the readings her students were supposed to pick up for that day's class. In spite of telling them in class to pick up the reading, and then taping a sign to her mailbox *reminding* them to pick the reading up when they dropped off their term papers, it looked like only a third of the articles had been picked up.

"I hate my students," Elizabeth said to her friend Madeline, who was in the office getting a cup of coffee. Madeline drove a bus for the local high school and sometimes brought the special ed kids over in the afternoon to use the college pool. Elizabeth had known Madeline since she was four. Her mother had gone through a gambling phase and would dump Elizabeth off at the same day-care center at the Indian casino where Madeline's father left her.

"This is my friend Lizzie," Madeline announced once to a security guard when they were about five. "I see her here every weekend." Neither of them realized what that said about their families until much later.

"What do you have in the box?" Madeline said now.

"A bird," Elizabeth said. "My cat got it this morning. Do you have a car?"

"Just the bus," said Madeline. "And I have to wait for my kids to get out of the locker rooms."

The bird began chirping loudly. Elizabeth gathered it up and took the extra readings to class.

Her students were sitting at their desks, dozing or talking on their cell phones. Elizabeth shut the door and wrote a pop quiz on the board.

"If you miss one question on this quiz," she said, "you will automatically fail."

"Peep! Peep! Peep!" said the bird.

The students squinted at her, surprised, since usually she was more friendly and hated to fail them. Even as she was saying this, Elizabeth knew she probably wouldn't count the Fs, but she liked the idea that she might. Saving the bird had given her this sort of reckless energy. Her hands were shaking, and she felt like she was on speed.

The students started writing, and Elizabeth stomped around, passing back papers and writing things on the board. Then she gave them a lecture.

"How did this happen?" she asked. "Did you not see the sign on my mailbox saying you were responsible for this reading? Did you not pay attention in class when I told you to pick up today's reading at my mailbox? Did you think for a second that in the business world a boss would accept 'I didn't see the giant memo you put on my desk' as an excuse?"

The students looked sad.

Elizabeth felt sad, too. The essay she had planned to teach that day was one of her favorites. It was about a Vietnamese girl who came to the U.S. with her parents after the Vietnam War. It was told in a series of vignettes, starting with a description of the narrator's mother, a daughter of a middle-class businessman, falling in love with the narrator's father, a rebel soldier, for his handsome face and his gentle hands.

Elizabeth loved this essay. She loved the way it depicted beauty in unlikely places, the defiance and longing in the narrator's voice. She loved the way the author talked about the shantytown where her family lived with the other immigrants and how most people looked at it and saw nothing but dirt and grime. "They haven't seen our gardens full of lemongrass, mint, cilantro, and basil," she had written. "Have they seen the berries we pick which turn our lips and fingertips red?"

And Elizabeth loved the end of the piece, when the narrator's family is forced to leave their new home, and her mother tells her father not to touch her with his gangster hands. The father punches the wall until his hands bleed, saying, "Let me see the gangster! Let me see his gangster hands." Elizabeth could not read this without crying. It killed her, the desperate, profound sense of loss in this marriage, how it illustrated the way we come to hate the things we once loved.

She put the bird down on her desk.

"Well," she said to her students. "For those of you

who actually prepared for class, what did you think?"

"This story was choppy," said Jimmy, a languid boy whose term paper had been called "Marijuana isn't to Bad."

"I was absent on Monday, so I didn't know what we were supposed to read," said Trevor, an ROTC student who had a terrible time following directions.

"Trevor," Elizabeth said. "It's your responsibility to find out what you missed when you're absent." He turned red and looked at his brick. For the past two weeks he'd been carrying around a light blue brick everywhere. "It's his rifle," Madeline told Elizabeth. "They're trying to teach them the responsibility of owning a gun."

"I was working on a paper for your class," he said glumly.

"I didn't get it," said a pretty, thin girl named Darlene. Darlene was a rodeo queen at sixteen and for her seventeenth birthday her mom took her out and they both came home with tattoos. "Why was everyone in it so angry?"

Normally, Elizabeth would have rolled with this. She would have discussed the immigrant experience. She would have tried to get them to see how each paragraph connected to the next. She would have shown them that this was an example of how to make a theme work, a perfect example of showing, not telling. But as she stood there, looking at them, their young, bored faces and perfect skin, she felt like banging her head into the chalkboard.

"Is that a bird in the box?" said Trevor.

"I took it from my cat's mouth this morning," Elizabeth said, "and I need to take it to the bird sanctuary after class."

Trevor was still looking at the box. "Why don't you just let nature run its course?" he said. "The cat can't help it."

"Isn't she, as a citizen, responsible for the actions of her cat?" said Darlene. She stretched in her chair, arching her back so that her breasts strained against her shirt, and Trevor blushed.

"Good critical thinking, Darlene," said Elizabeth.

"You should cancel class and take it out there now," said Jimmy. "It's going to need antibiotics. My cat gets birds every year."

Under most circumstances Elizabeth wouldn't have ended class early if her hair was on fire because she didn't want her students to think she was easy. But as she stood there, staring at them, thinking

about how they'd all rather be someplace else, it occurred to her that they probably already thought she
was easy. And then she thought, Well, maybe I am.
"I'll end class early if one of you will drive me to the
bird sanctuary," she said.

Trevor raised his hand.

Elizabeth knew she shouldn't get into the car with
Trevor. She remembered the three things she'd been
told in her teacher training course not to do if she
wanted to maintain her authority. One: Don't erase
the board from side to side—your butt will jiggle and
the students will laugh at you. Two: Don't make self-
deprecating jokes. Three: Don't invite the students to
your house, and never, ever get into a car with them.
They are not your friends and driving with them will
cause all kinds of boundary issues. She knew that she
could lose her job for asking a student to drive her
anywhere. But then she decided, Who cares? I found
this bird, and I am going to goddamn save it.

Trevor wanted to talk to her anyway because he
was having trouble with his third paper, which was
supposed to be a persuasive essay.

"Have you come up with a topic?" she asked. His
second paper had been about how he'd had to lose
thirty-five pounds in two weeks to pass the army

physical. He ate only salad, fruit, and water. He wore a plastic-lined suit and two pairs of socks, and drove his car around with the windows rolled up and the heat on in the middle of summer. When he took the physical, he made the weight requirement, but his pee was orange. They took him anyway, but by the time he got to basic training he'd gained back his water weight, so they sent him to the unit for the "unfit," where he was locked up with drug addicts and psychotics and spent each day scrubbing pigeon shit off the sidewalks. Elizabeth had loved this essay, and suggested that he write the next one on practices in the army, or maybe how certain sports encourage the same kind of eating disorders in men that modeling causes in women."

But Trevor had other ideas. "I want to use history, logic, and archaeological evidence to prove that Jesus really is the Messiah," Trevor said now.

Elizabeth's blood began to pound. She got this paper every quarter. Every quarter she wrote on the board that a thesis statement was supposed to be unified, debatable, and supportable; therefore, you should not write about a belief. And every quarter some kid wanted to write about Jesus. "That's a belief," she said. "How are you going to support it?"

"I'm going to use historical and logical evidence," Trevor said.

A knot of frustration tightened in her stomach, the same one she got when she looked at all her students wearing Abercrombie & Fitch and telling her they weren't affected by advertising. "Even if we have evidence that Jesus lived," Elizabeth said, "that doesn't necessarily make him the Messiah." Trevor stared straight ahead. His father was German-American and his mother Vietnamese, and Elizabeth was struck, as she often was in class, by just how handsome he was.

"Isn't that a belief?" he said.

"What?"

"Aren't you believing He's *not* the Messiah?"

"I'm not writing a paper on it," she said.

"The trouble with a belief is that it locks you in," Elizabeth went on. "Writing is all about excavating. The best papers explore all the different sides of a topic or situation, even the parts that are hard to deal with."

Trevor made an uncomfortable face, as if she were slowly and persistently poking him in the side.

"For example," Elizabeth said. "What if you had a friend and you had known him for years and then one day you found out that once he slept with a man?"

"Um," Trevor said. "What do you mean?"

"Then you would know more about that character. It might change the way you look at him, or how you see yourself."

"My ex-girlfriend kissed another girl once," Trevor said.

"It's different for girls," Elizabeth said.

"Yes," Trevor said. "It's hotter."

They drove around a curve and the bottle of water thumped in the box with the bird in it. Elizabeth opened the lid. The bird blinked at her as if to say, *Why am I in this stupid box? I want a worm. How could you not know your husband was gay?*

"Why don't you write about how being a born-again Christian is as much of a leap of faith as being an atheist?" said Elizabeth.

"I'll go to hell," Trevor said.

He said it with such certainty, such blind faith that things would go the way he thought they would, that Elizabeth wanted to shake him.

"Oh, for God's sake, Trevor," she said. "Do you really think all Jews and Buddhists are going to hell? Do you think I'm going to hell? I'm sitting here with a baby bird on my lap that I rescued from being eaten alive. I ride my bike to and from school to save on fuel. I recycle. You're carrying a blue brick that's supposed to be your rifle. And you think I'm going to hell and you're not?"

Trevor turned red and kept his eyes on the road.

"Yes, ma'am," he said.

"Let me ask you something," Elizabeth said. "What made you want to be saved? What made you think you're so terrible that you need Jesus to save you?"

Trevor said nothing.

"How old are you, eighteen?" she said. She could feel her face getting hot. "What could you have done? Masturbated? Taken money from your parents?" They passed a dead, bloated raccoon lying on its back on the roadside, its little arms and legs splayed out.

"I bet you kissed a boy," she said.

Trevor flushed.

"I bet you kissed a boy and you want Jesus to save you from yourself."

"Mrs. Teeter," Trevor said, "are you mad at me?"

They pulled into the parking lot of the Wildlife Center, and he stopped the car. "It seems as though you're attacking me personally, and I'm just trying to talk about my paper."

"You're all so afraid of sex," she said. "Sex before marriage is bad, sex with a same-sex person is bad.

I'll tell you what's really bad. What's really bad is when you're married to someone and you just don't like having sex with him at all. Have you thought about that?"

Trevor was looking at his hands. They were strong hands with graceful fingers, the kind Elizabeth loved on a man. "No, ma'am," he said. "Not like that."

"You don't think," she said. "None of you do."

Elizabeth put her head in her hands. She imagined that later Trevor would complain to his mother and possibly the Moral Majority that she had overstepped all her boundaries. She'd lose her job and have no husband and spend the rest of her life sitting in her house trying to control her stupid cat. She'd be attracted to other men and they'd probably all be gay and eventually she'd find a woman who was just like her father who would leave her, too.

"I haven't kissed a boy," Trevor said. "My brother is gay, but I don't like guys that way."

The bird, which had gotten very quiet, rustled a little in its fake nest.

"Remember how in my last essay I wrote about that place I had to stay?" Trevor said. "There was a guy who was in there because someone said he was a homosexual and we all gave him a really bad time.

One day we locked him in a locker and peed all over him and left him there."

Elizabeth didn't look up, and for a moment all she could think was, for Christ's sake, Trevor, why didn't you write about that?

"Then later that night he slit his own throat with a shaving razor. He was right next to me and I couldn't think of what to do so I reached over and held his throat together with my hands. I tried to talk to him. I told him that we would all get out of there soon so he should hold on. I don't know if he noticed because he was pretty far gone. But I held on and all I kept thinking was, Please, dear God, please take this job away from me. Someone else take this job."

Elizabeth's head was still down in her hands, and she was afraid if she started to cry she would never stop. She wanted Trevor to kiss her. She wanted his beautiful, sad hands on her neck, in her hair. "Please," she prayed silently, "let him kiss me." She knew that if she was going to pray she should be praying for Trevor, or that poor dead boy, or even the baby bird. And she also knew that kissing Trevor would be futile, that it would only disappoint her and confuse him, and both of them would end up sadder than they already were.

She could hear cars whirring by the Wildlife Center, which was in the middle of a strip mall. "Please," she prayed again. "I need to kiss someone."

Trevor took the key out of the ignition. "It's how I make sense of things," he said. "It may not work for you, but it's what I know."

She heard him undo his seat belt. He leaned toward her, close enough that she could smell his young, salty skin. She wanted him to touch her so much her heart actually stopped. But he didn't. Instead, he very gently took the box with the bird in it from her hands. Then he picked up his blue brick, got out of the car, and when she lifted her head he was walking away from her to the Wildlife Center, bird in one hand and fake rifle in the other.

INSTRUCTIONS FOR
A SUBSTITUTE BUS DRIVER

From the desk of: Madeline Harris

The bus route is shaped roughly like the state of Nevada, a big square with a smaller triangle attached. You start on Stuyvesant Hill, where the children of professors, lawyers, and doctors live in updated houses separated by hedgerows or narrow gardens. You'll drop off Jeannie Kamine, who carves her initials into the freckled flesh of her upper arm. You'll let off Robbie Bartin, a fourth-grader with a paste-eating problem, and Doug Palumbo, whose mother gave him a perm and who's good at math and who has such terrible breath that his face, beautiful, like that of a young Paul Newman, goes unnoticed.

On the back of the bus the high school boys lounge like panthers, same as it is on all the buses. My advice to you is to separate them from the pack if you need to discipline them. Stop the bus, take them off, talk to them man-to-man, even if you're a woman. Humiliate them in front of their friends, and it's over. On this route the ringleaders in the back are John Gretsky and LeRoy Rat—the boys who talk about sex and make out with their girlfriends, putting their jackets over their heads for privacy, even though everyone knows what's going on under there.

In the middle sit the stoners, who don't really care about anything, along with the kids who want to stay out of trouble. Annette McConkey, with her pale skin and nervous hands; plain Betty Reilly, who does her homework the whole time the bus is moving; Jill Goodman, with the braces, who according to the grapevine (a kid named Jerry Fry) threatened her mother with a knife; and Ruby Plumadore, the chubby one who absently taps her fingers on the window, as if she is waving goodbye to someone, or is already gone.

The front is where the special ed kids sit, along

with Jerry Fry, who loves the bus and will tell you where to stop. Jerry's a small kid who excels in baton twirling and home ec and wears to school an outfit he made himself that makes him look like a little French schoolboy. He'll grow up and do well for himself, in a place like New York or San Francisco, but it's hard for a boy like him to be small and in seventh grade in a place like this. And Jerry doesn't make things easier on himself. Most kids in his position would try not to be noticed, but Jerry not only does what he can to get attention, he insults the people who give it to him. If someone makes fun of his schoolboy outfit, he'll make fun of their sneakers, or say something like "Wrestling is for fags, douche wipe," and then he'll get punched in the face, or someone will steal his knapsack.

Last week Jerry told me that John Gretsky was showing a group of fifth graders a *Penthouse* magazine he'd stolen from his dad. John is the middle and best-looking of three sons belonging to Marty Gretsky, who runs an illegal cockfighting ring on his property. He's has a lean face with full lips and dirty blond hair that falls over his eyes. He's always on the verge of dropping out of school and has been suspended twice, once for carrying a slingshot, another time for bringing porn to biology class. Before the

Penthouse incident, he was showing everyone a wart he said he got from his girlfriend. This, too, I heard from Jerry.

"John's back there showing everyone a wart he has on his hand," Jerry said. He was wearing a hairstyle that appeared to be inspired by Prince Valiant. "He says his girlfriend has them on her vagina and that's how he got one on his thumb."

"Gross!" said Katie Lane, who was sitting on the other side of Jerry and has Asperger's syndrome.

You got that right, I thought, and then I thought, Who says *vagina* in seventh grade? Kid, I wanted to say to Jerry, you'll do a lot better in this place if you call it a pussy or a hair pie.

After you finish on Stuyvesant Hill, you drive north, where the land opens up and the houses are separated by wheat fields and pastures. You'll drive by the swath of sunflowers and the Shattucks' strawberry fields. You'll let off J. R. Lutz, who smells like cows and sits alone, and then the Mulvaneys, a family of five sleepy-eyed farm boys with big hands. Every year one of the boys gets someone pregnant, and a blotchy-skinned girl with a swollen waistline will show up at their bus stop because she's been kicked out of her own home and has to live with them. Mrs. Mulvaney takes them all in, even though she's never had much use for girls. This year it's a sophomore named Lorraine, a timid, spidery-legged girl who always wears a poncho.

I was driving Luther Hawk's route in the afternoon, which was Lorraine's bus, the day her father found out she was pregnant. She got off the bus and I heard a door slam, and I saw her father come out of the house, walking fast, hands moving like pistons. I could hear him yelling at her through the window, "whore," and "stupid cow," and then when he got to her, he shoved her so hard she fell to her knees. The kids got quiet, and I shifted into gear and pulled away. When I looked in the rearview mirror, I saw Lorraine sitting on the ground, shoulders hunched, and her father standing above her, staring uselessly at his hands.

Two days later she was on my bus. You could see a bruise, a blooming purple stain, on her otherwise ordinary face.

I've never liked her father, Jack, who spends most of his time at the diner complaining that nobody wants to work while his wife runs the farm. And I still don't like him. But a tiny part of me felt sorry for him that day, although of course I felt worse for Lorraine. Some children are lost to you for reasons you don't know. Even the ones that smile and seem so easy in the first part of their lives can turn surly and unreachable. My daughter changed almost overnight. She was a dream child, happy and smart, and then when she turned twelve it was like a train hit our whole family. She dyed her brown hair a shrieking shade of blond, started smoking, and treated me and her father like dirt. If I grounded her, she climbed out a window; if her father stopped giving her an allowance, she stole his money. We ended up hiding the checkbook and our wallets behind a tile in the ceiling. Her father and I—this was before the divorce—didn't know why she was acting this way. I had my theories. Now she's training to be a counselor, and she would agree with them. She'll say that she was an oedipal child, that she was trying to break from him and destroy me, and hanging out with drug addicts, stealing our money, walking through the house topless, et cetera was the only way she knew how to do it.

Keep an eye on Marcy Pierce, the redhead the boys on the back of the bus call Fire Crotch. She used to sit in the middle of the bus, but a few weeks ago Leroy Rat jumped some seats and sat behind her.

He started sweet-talking her, telling her she was so pretty, he couldn't believe someone as pretty as her lived in this town. It reminded me of a box of letters I'd found in my daughter's room after she moved out. They were from a guy she was seeing who was in jail for statutory rape. Every page was full of lines about how special Susie was, how there was no one else in the world like her, how she was the only one for him. Everything a girl that age wants to believe someone can think about her, only her, and every line the same one he gave to someone else.

Last week Marcy was sitting closer to the back, and a few days ago she disappeared under Leroy's jacket. Jerry Fry went to investigate and came back to tell me that Leroy had his hand down her pants. I stopped the bus and separated them, but you know these kids. They don't stay apart for very long. You have to keep an eye on them every minute. But who wants to know what they're doing?

I thought my daughter was just going through a rebellious stage, and then one day she called me at the bus garage to say she was at the clinic getting an abortion. I didn't even think she was having sex. Who wants to think about that? Teenage sex is so revolting. I know. I did it myself. And you know it, too, if you drive a school bus. The bus is such a jangly petri dish of kids groping their way through adolescence. They don't quite know what sex means yet, but they act like they do, calling each other names like Fire Crotch, talking about genital warts, giving each other twisted advice as if they know what they're talking about. And the worst part is, a few of them do.

When my daughter called that day, I didn't know what to do. I asked her if she wanted me to come down to the clinic and she said she didn't know. It was going to happen soon, she said, and by the time I got down there she'd probably be done.

I got off the phone and stood there, breathing in the familiar smells of exhaust, oil, and Luther Hawk's aftershave. I figured some part of her must have wanted me to go down there or she wouldn't have called, but then the rest of her was so angry at us then, I didn't know if me being there would just make things worse. And I'm pro-choice, but I think abortions are terrible things, and she knew that. I ended up calling my mother-in-law. She was a strict Catholic and had about twelve kids, but I always felt like she understood what to do in situations like this. She said, "Oh, honey. Go be with your daughter. If I were in your shoes, that's what I would do."

So I went. I got to the clinic and Susie's boyfriend Sammy was there, sitting on a hard plastic chair, knees far apart, chewing on a pencil. I asked him how she was, and he said she was fine, she was already in the operating room. I always got along well with Sammy, and we sat there for a while. We didn't say much, just waited, and after about an hour she came out. She looked scared and relieved, both, and so young. I was sad looking at her. Sad that the baby was gone, sad that my daughter had been so ashamed she couldn't come to me, that she had to make a decision like that herself. She hugged Sam, and then she hugged me, although she was so stiff in my arms it was like hugging bark. I said, "How are you doing?" and she said she was all right. Then I asked her if she was ready to go home, and she said, "I'm not going home, Mom." Then she looked at Sammy and said, "Let's go."

I'll admit I was hurt by that. Actually, I felt like I'd been punched in the throat.

A mile from the strawberry fields is John Gretsky's house. The porch needs paint and is piled with junk, and an assortment of feral dogs run the property.

John's father is on disability for an irate temper, and his mother is sedated most of the time. Last month they drove into a ditch and totaled the car but crawled out of the mess drunk and still fighting.

After the Gretskys' house, you turn and drive the smaller triangular section, going back farther into the hills to the worn-out trailers with rusted swing sets and tar-papered doghouses, where the children who are treated most unfairly finally get off the bus. This is the part of the route that gets me the most. Not just because of the landscape, which is dramatic and full of wild sky, but because of the rough houses, the cars on the front lawns, the way the children who live here seem so much older than they are. You watch a kid like Ruby Plumadore, whose clothes never fit and who smells like cigarettes, whose hair snarls around her head like a galaxy, get off the bus and walk up her driveway, and you see her subtly gird herself to walk into her front door. You can't help thinking, It shouldn't be that hard to be a child. I didn't have an easy time growing up either, but I had a kind neighbor and a strong aunt, and some of these kids seem to have nothing.

The run-down A-frame set back from the road is

where you let off Jerry Fry. His mother waits for him by the front window. I see her every weekday, smoking Virginia Slims with bony fingers. I wonder what she thinks as she watches her odd little boy, already stoop-shouldered from the weight of the other kids' insults, get off the bus, stop to get the mail, and then turn to give everyone on the bus the finger.

Does she root for him? Does she wonder what to do with a kid who consistently asks for love the wrong way?

My then-husband and I didn't talk about our daughter's abortion for weeks. Then finally one night he asked me how I was doing. "I'm managing," I said. "You?"

"I feel like I'm grieving," he said. We had spent the afternoon cutting and stacking wood, and sawdust clung to his hair. "But it's not like anyone died."

A thin line of dirt had settled into the crease of his neck, and I wiped it away. Then I left my hand there on his skin, just below his ear. I felt sorry for him. The world isn't set up to keep men company the way it is for women. I carried babies, and I know what it's like, how you can feel them floating in the blackness of your insides, rolling, waving at you with their starfish hands. We're more connected to being alive this way, while men, I think, are always a little unmoored.

"Our first grandchild did," I said.

The last stop is Betty Reilly's, an old clapboard farmhouse set back in the woods. Betty reminds me of myself at her age—her matter-of-fact manner, her steady, determined walk. Her mother is a beekeeper and her father was Amish until he met and fell in love with her mother. I often wonder if it's because of this that the three of them seem like such a tight, sturdy unit, unbreakable as the chairs Betty's father hand crafts from oak. Betty will take a moment to gather her things and as she passes you, she'll tell you to have a good night. She does this without fail. "Have a good night," she'll say. Then she'll get off the bus and walk up her driveway, eyes to the ground, oblivious to the dark, wild beauty surrounding her home.

EYE. ARM. LEG. HEART.

It was his liver, hardened by five thousand gallons of eighty-proof gin, that finally killed Harlin Wilder.

The sudden burst of loneliness Grace Meyers felt when she heard this news caught her off guard. Her on-again, off-again carrying-on with Harlin had ended years ago, and Grace had long since put that time behind her. Still, when Harlin's lawyer, Lanford Guthrie, showed up at the house she grew up in and told her Harlin was dead, she sat down on her mother's front porch and put her head in her hands.

"It's a sad thing." Lanford, who was a polite man, took a miniature bottle of whiskey out of his coat pocket and handed it to her. "They don't make them like Harlin anymore."

Grace felt the liquid go down and remembered how much she liked whiskey. She had given up hard liquor and cigarettes a few years before, after she'd found a lump in her breast, but she missed her old bad habits. Now, the whiskey warming her blood, she looked at the barn across the street, sagging in the middle as if it understood her. It had been over a year since her mother had died, and Grace had only just now gotten around to clearing out the last of her things so she could sell the house. It seemed as if life was moving too fast, as if too many people were leaving it, and now Harlin, too, was gone for good.

Lanford took off his jacket and put it neatly on the porch next to him. "I represented him in court a while ago," he said. "His wife was suing him because he took all her money to start up a petting zoo."

"What in the hell was he going to do with a petting zoo?" Grace said. She took another sip of whiskey and handed the bottle back to Lanford. Even as she said it, she knew exactly what Harlin would do with a petting zoo. He had always been a ridiculous optimist, certain that he could make a lot of money if he could just find the right plan. "Let's go to Bermuda and make a million bucks chartering boats," he'd say. "Let's take that Airstream and make

it into a coffee shop. What about a drive-through grocery?" They weren't all bad ideas; some of them were
very good, which was the worst part, since they all
overlooked the fact that Harlin had terrible credit
and very little follow-through.

"He got drunk one day and decided he was going
to start this zoo out at his dad's old place," Lanford
said. He was thin and wiry, with a bony, dignified
face and thick dark curls that were graying at the
base of his neck. "He took Charlene's money out of
her savings and spent it all on fencing supplies and
animal feed."

"And beer for all the people he was going to hire,"
Grace said.

Lanford smiled. "Naturally," he said.

"Including you," she said. She meant to laugh
when she said this, but then she began to cry. She
had loved Harlin, and he had loved her, and even
though all that time had passed, she remembered his
voice and his hands, and the way he couldn't get
enough of her skin.

"I'm sorry," she said. "I just expected him to live a
little longer."

Lanford let her cry. He had known her since third
grade, when he was a crier himself, and knew there

was no shame in it. He put his arm around her shoulders, and Grace could smell good whiskey and cigarettes, a smell she'd always liked on a man. She breathed it in from his shirt before she pulled away.

Lanford took a cocktail napkin out of his pocket and checked it for phone numbers. Seeing none, he handed it to Grace, who took it. His hands were thin like his face, but callused, which was both surprising and appealing in a lawyer.

"They had the funeral out at the hospital, but the wake is tomorrow," he said.

"Are you going?" Grace guessed the answer even before Lanford shook his head. The service would be full of his clients, and Grace knew Lanford, who saw a little bit of himself in each one, wouldn't want to be closer to their lives than he already was.

"No," Lanford said. "But Cyrus Wilder was out last night telling everyone it was going to be a big party."

Grace laughed and blew her nose. "I bet he was."

Lanford picked up his coat and draped it over his arm.

"It's nice to see you, Grace," he said. "You should come see me after the wake if you go."

It was a pass and Grace knew it, and she thought

about reminding him that she was living with a cabinetmaker named Trey several towns south. But then she decided not to insult him. Her boyfriend didn't matter to him any more than any man she dated outside her hometown mattered to anyone there, and it was rare these days that anyone, even Trey, looked at her the way Lanford was looking at her now, like she was a single, ripe piece of fruit.

"You're sweet to try, Lanford Guthrie," she said.

"Nothing sweet about it," he said and left.

The wake was held the next day at the Elks' Lodge, a square, brick building with stingy windows across the street from the Royal Court Inn, where Grace had booked a room to avoid the barrenness of her mother's house. From the window she watched people filing in: Two men staggered up the steps, possibly drunk. Three more, hair slicked down and side-parted, wore clean work pants and button-down shirts and carried containers of food. A mother with three wild-haired children appeared with a coffee urn, and another woman who looked like she could lift a piano carried a cooler of beer. She wore her black hair up in a haphazard knot, no eye makeup, and lots of lipstick on wonderful bright red lips. She was followed by someone Grace recognized—Rita, the bartender from Lucy's Tavern, where Grace and Harlin used to drink. Grace guessed that the black-haired woman was Rita's girlfriend. So that's what she looks like, she thought. Not bad.

There were a few more faces Grace recognized—Harlin's cousin Earl, wearing thick glasses and carrying what looked like a conga drum; and Hank Stevens, who couldn't drive because of the metal plate in his head and rode in on his bicycle. Stewart Levine showed up, too, wearing a brown corduroy suit whose pants barely reached his ankles and carrying a fistful of balloons that said "Congratulations." Cyrus Wilder, Harlin's older brother by fifteen minutes and the only one of four sons left, walked up the stairs wearing a neck brace, his arm around on his ex-wife, Janet. Martin Pugliese sidled in, too, followed by two other men in ill-fitting suits who Grace guessed were members of Cyrus's band.

The rest of the faces, however, were only vaguely familiar, and Grace was reminded that it had been a long time since she'd been back in this part of her hometown. She guessed that a lot of the people she used to know from drinking with Harlin had, like her, moved on. She'd heard that Linda Hartley had gone to Hawaii, and Benny Jackson had retired to North Carolina to be closer to his son. Austin Jones had moved to Canada and married a nurse, and Bill Kane had quit drinking and shacked up with Madeline Harris.

Grace poured herself a shot of bourbon, straight up, something Harlin had taught her to do. It was important for a woman, he'd always said, to know what she was drinking, not to dress it up in juices and tonics so that she forgot what she was doing. She drank the bourbon in Harlin's honor, smoothed down her black skirt, and crossed the street to his wake.

In the lodge basement, Harlin's mourners arranged themselves in small groups. Some stood, but most of them sat at long cafeteria-style tables, with cans of Budweiser and plates of cold cuts, baked beans, and scalloped potatoes that had come from tinfoil pans and were set out at the front of the room. In the back of the room was a cake with a picture on it of the waterfall out near the power plant, where Harlin, according to his brother and the police officers present, often went to get stoned.

Grace stood in the doorway, taking in the room.

Most of the people she knew were busy. Rita was in the back helping with the food, and Stewart, who never remembered her even when they were drinking together, was standing with Cyrus Wilder and Martin Pugliese, getting their pictures taken as if they were all at a wedding. It was Ada Wilder, Harlin's younger sister, who finally approached her.

"Grace," she said, taking Grace's hands into her own, which were small, like Harlin's. "I haven't seen you in a million years."

Grace smiled. "Ada," she said. "I didn't recognize you." Ada wore a loose-fitting green linen dress, and her hair had gone back to its natural color and condition, which was straight and brown. The last time Grace had seen her she was blond and at a volunteer firemen's clambake, where she'd asked if Grace thought twenty-five dollars was enough to charge a guy for letting him see her boobs. ("Ask for a hundred, settle for thirty-five," Grace had said.)

Ada led Grace to a table where two men and a woman sat eating macaroni salad from paper plates and drinking beer. They were all young—the men hard-boned with farmers' caps and jackets that smelled like wood smoke. The woman had the smooth brown skin and wavy dark hair of an Indian-

European mix. Harlin's sister introduced the men as Rusty and Jack. She didn't introduce the woman, and Grace remembered that this was something she'd always disliked about Ada.

"Grace grew up near here," Ada said. "She was married to Harlin for a short time."

The small group of mourners must have liked Grace—perhaps they wanted to honor a wife of the deceased, or maybe they liked her face, which had softened over the years—but they immediately tried to make her feel comfortable. They cleared a space for her at the table, and Jack, the rougher looking of the two men, got up to get her a beer. The woman, who introduced herself as Anne-Marie, offered her a cheese cube and some crackers. Grace accepted and settled in, and asked them how they all knew Harlin.

Jack said he'd met him working on a road crew out in Newfield. And Rusty said his birth mother had lived next to Harlin when he was a baby, but that he'd gotten to know Harlin at the horse auctions a few years back. Grace imagined the boy was good with horses. He was a handsome kid, thin but muscular, as if he lifted boxes of coal for a living. His skin was a deep reddish brown as if he had some Indian blood in him, and there was a vulnerability about his expression and unkempt hair that she imagined put people and animals at ease.

Grace told them she'd met Harlin at Lucy's Tavern, where they used to drink together. Jack wondered out loud if there was any other place in the world Harlin could meet a woman. Probably jail, Grace said. Maybe a hospital. They all laughed except for Anne-Marie, who said she didn't really know Harlin at all. Her fiancé, Martin Pugliese, knew him, which was why she was here, only he'd gone off a while ago to smoke a cigarette, so now she was all alone.

The two men ignored this last statement, if they even noticed it, and Rusty turned to Grace. "And you were married to Harlin?" he said.

Grace shook her head. "For a very short time," she said. "But then we were on-again, off-again for about ten years."

"Ten years," said Rusty. "Man. I think his last wife could only put up with him for five."

Grace laughed. "That's why I didn't stay married to him."

Warmed by the beer and the man they had in common, the group began to talk more about Harlin. They told story after story of hard luck, lost jobs, the time Harlin almost killed a friend of his with a broken beer bottle, the house he accidentally set on fire. Jack picked at the Agway logo on his farmer's cap and said he couldn't believe Harlin was actually dead. He'd always thought Harlin was the kind of drunk who kept on living long after all the joggers had heart attacks and those fucking hippie vegans came down with stomach cancer. Long after the kidneys and livers of any normal drinkers gave up for good.

Grace nodded and said she'd felt that way about him, too. She told them about the time Harlin rode his motorcycle into Lucy's Tavern because it was brand-new and he couldn't wait for her to see it. Anne-Marie told a story her fiancé had told her, about a time Harlin put on an Easter bonnet to be part of a parade one of the women at the bar had organized. Rusty told a story about Harlin pulling his nephew out of a car wreck when his hands were bleeding and his own ribs were fractured.

Grace remembered that accident, and how Harlin was afraid to drive for months afterward.

"Did you ever hear him sing?" she said. "He could sound like Hank Williams if he wanted to. There was so much longing in that voice. People cried when he sang."

"It was his singing that got him evicted from his

last apartment," Rusty said. "That and a few other things." He reached into Jack's knapsack and pulled out a bottle of Southern Comfort. Jack noticed and frowned, but Rusty opened it anyway and said, "It's for the ladies."

Rusty began pouring shots into foam cups, and Anne-Marie asked Grace if she wanted to see a picture of her daughter. She reached into her purse and pulled out a picture of a little girl who, she said, did not belong to her fiancé, Martin. Good, Grace thought. She had never liked Martin, with his girly legs and squinty face. How a man like that got a woman to agree to spend two minutes, let alone the rest of her life, with him was beyond her.

"That's a beautiful child," Grace said.

"I know," Anne-Marie said. "I'm having another one, too, which is why I'm so fat." She pulled out a photocopy of a sonogram, where a ghostly white shadow floated against a black background. Someone had drawn arrows to different points on the figure and written in careful block letters: "Eye." "Arm." "Leg."

"That's beautiful, too," Grace said. She was getting drunk. On just one shot of bourbon and a beer. A disgrace to her old self, she thought.

"You can't see what it looks like yet," Anne-Marie said a bit crossly. "Its father"—she gestured toward the door—"is part German and a little Italian. I'm part Cherokee and part Cajun."

"Might as well have your own goddamn continent in there," mumbled Jack.

"You're an asshole," Anne-Marie said and tenderly smoothed the photocopy of her sonogram as if it were already a child.

"Harlin had a kid," Grace said. The guests looked at her with mild surprise, except for Rusty, who was busy trying to catch the eye of a girl with a nose ring a few tables over. "A daughter," Grace continued, "probably the same age as you boys he ended up partying with. Isn't that funny?"

"Harlin just wanted to stay young," Jack said, his tone treading the line between defensive and offensive. "He liked to hang with guys who knew how to party."

Anne-Marie looked at him in a soft way, the way you might look at a soldier going off to fight an unwinnable war. "Oh, honey," she said. "By funny, she meant pathetic."

"I think his daughter's a cop in Wyoming now," Grace said. She did a quick scan of the room to see if anyone looking remotely like Harlin's girl were there but saw no one.

Harlin's sister Ada got up to lead the group in prayer, and after she sat down Harlin's brother Cyrus stood up to make a toast.

"Cyrus," Ada said. "It's too early!"

But Cyrus insisted he had something to say and banged his jackknife on a foam cup until the group quieted down.

"There was a lot you could say about Harlin," Cyrus began. "He went too far sometimes, and made some bad decisions. But Harlin was responsible for the mood in any bar. If he was drinking and the drinking was good, he could light up a place."

Harlin, Cyrus continued, had learned the right lessons in jail. He committed some crimes, did his time, and when he got out he wanted to be remembered as a gentle man. He paused and adjusted his neck brace.

"It wasn't an easy thing to do," he went on. "Harlin had a violent nature." There was a low grumble of agreement in the crowd.

"But there was something in Harlin that always made you want to help him," Cyrus said. "You couldn't not forgive him. He had this kindness, a sort of wisdom. Harlin always knew what was eating you whether you told him or not."

Grace took another drink from her foam cup. She considered the times she had forgiven Harlin: for the other women, his jealousy, the things he forgot, like her birthday, his car payments. No man had made her as angry as Harlin did, but no one had ever apologized the way he did either. "I'm so sorry," he'd said, after she caught him feeling up Linda Hartley in the alley behind Lucy's. "It's just that she reminded me of you, and you weren't there."

That bastard, she thought now. The worst part was that he meant it.

Cyrus sat down and Harlin's cousin Earl, round-faced and long-limbed, stood.

"Harlin gave me this drum," Earl said, holding up a brown conga drum, stretched tight with some kind of hide.

"He loved nature," Earl continued. "So if you see me with this drum, you can come up and say hello to Harlin." He sat down.

There was laughter and a few amens, and then conversations picked up again, slowly at first, then busy like the drone of bees. At her table, Grace poured herself another shot of Southern Comfort. "A

drum made of animal skin isn't exactly kind to nature," she said.

"He did love animals, though," said Rusty.

"Oh, sure he did," Grace said. "You know why his
last wife was suing him? He took all her money to
start a petting zoo at his father's house." Her face felt
flushed, and Anne-Marie patted her hand.

"There wasn't anything out there," Grace said.
"Some mean dogs, a few roosters, and a goat. A child
would get mange or rabies going to a place like
that." She realized she sounded angry, but so what?
Who wouldn't be upset by the loss of a man she'd
loved enough to take back and throw out for ten
years?

"He was an entrepreneur," Jack said. "A free spirit."

"It's a lot easier to be a free spirit when someone
else is cleaning up the mess," said Grace.

"That's so true," said Anne-Marie and excused herself to go get her fiancé, Martin, who was threatening
to punch Ada's husband in the eye.

"They'll last about three weeks," muttered Jack.

"She's not bad looking, though," said Rusty. They
sat quietly for a minute, picking at their food.

"What about you?" Jack said. "Are you married?"

Grace showed him her ringless left hand. "I did

that a bunch of times," she said. "Now I just live with someone."

"I'm getting a divorce," Jack said. "So's he." He shrugged a shoulder toward Rusty.

"I love my wife," said Rusty. "We're about to have a little baby."

"You love your wife," Jack corrected. "But you aren't in love with her."

"No, I'm in love with her," Rusty said. "You never know, things might work out."

He looked at Grace, as if asking for her permission to have this hope.

"They might," she said, granting it.

Jack asked Grace if she wanted to see a picture of his son. He opened his wallet and pulled out a snapshot of a tiny blond boy with huge cheeks, his face covered in something brown.

"Why do you even show people that picture?" said Rusty. "Your kid looks filthy."

"That's when we were down in Florida," Jack said, ignoring Rusty. "That's chili on his face. He loves that stuff."

"Florida?" Grace said, surprised. Jack looked like the kind of guy who got up every day, went to a job washing dishes or working at a gas station, got wasted at night, and drove around in his car. He looked like the kind of guy who would never leave town, wouldn't even want to, because there were too many assholes in the world and he had enough to deal with in his own county. She had grown up with people like that, always complaining about how much the place sucked. Never leaving it.

"My wife wanted us to live near her family," he said, picking at some facial hair that was growing in no particular order on his chin. "But I got drunk and got into a fight with her dad and now we're back here."

"I can't fight when I'm drunk," said Rusty. "I get too mean. I'm a little guy, but I can drink about a case. And when I'm in a bad mood on top of that . . ." He shrugged as if to say, Who knew what would happen?

"Yeah, he drinks and he passes out," Jack said. "Then he gets his second wind and he'll pick a fight with someone three times his size."

"I don't even know what I do," said Rusty. He smiled apologetically, and Grace noticed that one of his teeth was broken at an angle, which made him look cunning. "My wife gets real mad at me."

"I would get mad at you, too, if I was your wife," Grace said.

"Yeah," Rusty said. "But you have a nice personality. My wife doesn't. She's mean."

"She's vindictive," said Jack.

"She ran off with five guys," said Rusty. He looked at Grace as if he still couldn't believe it, then back at his foam cup.

"I still love her, though," he said. "I knew we'd have problems. That's why I married her right away. She was only eighteen, but I married her after I'd only known her for three months." He played with the sleeve of his shirt. The cuff was dirty, but Grace noticed his fingernails were flat and clean. "I don't know," he said. "We'll see when the baby comes. But I'm paying child support no matter what. She's my first wife and I'm her first husband and I want to do right by her."

"I married Harlin because I knew we'd have problems," Grace said. She said this because she wanted to make him feel less alone, but as she spoke she realized that it was true. She'd known right away that she and Harlin would never make it as a married couple. She could see the trouble before it started happening, the promises he'd never be able to keep, how it was never his fault when he got yelled at at work, the way she couldn't help flirting with other men when she was with him. Grace, a practical woman at heart, knew this was no good. But one night he'd taken her face in his hands and said, "I could never get tired of looking at you." She knew he would, that she was not beautiful in that way, and that he was drunk enough he might not even remember this the next morning. But to be looked at like that, she thought. If I give this up now, will anyone ever look at me this way again? So she'd married him, just to keep that for a while.

"Yeah," Rusty said. "It doesn't really work though. I bought her a thousand-dollar ring and everything, but she wore it on a trampoline and the prongs got bent and the diamond won't stay in. I don't know. I have to find another girl, because she's all I think about, and I can't be thinking about that anymore. I just need someone to be with." He pushed his chair a little closer to Grace.

Jack said he wanted someone to be with, too, someone he could hold all night and then get up and make her breakfast, and Rusty told him he was full of shit. "You can't even make breakfast for your own kid, let alone a woman."

Jack made a very crude gesture involving his crotch.

"He's a bad cook," Rusty said to Grace. "He smokes too much and can't smell anything. You can't cook if you can't smell anything."

"Trey, the man I live with, is a great cook," Grace said. It was a tactic she used to use at the bar, when men complained hungrily to her about their wives— bringing up another man. It never ceased to amaze her how this always made her more attractive. "He cooks and he cleans, which is lucky, because I'm a slob."

"You know what you can do," said Rusty helpfully. "If you have a glass of something, pick it up and take it with you the next time you go into the kitchen."

"Don't leave stuff behind the bathroom door," said Jack.

"I fucking hate that," said Rusty.

"I always do that," Grace said. "I take my clothes off, take a shower, and then go into the bedroom to get dressed, and the dirty clothes stay in the bathroom." It occurred to her that maybe she shouldn't be talking about taking her clothes off to two men half her age. Then it occurred to her that no, that was exactly what she should be doing, especially at Harlin's funeral.

"Take your clothes with you," said Jack. "Or put them in a hamper."

"You can make a chore list," added Rusty.

The crowd of mourners had finished eating and had begun to relax, stretching arms across the backs of chairs, loosing belts and ties. Stewart Levine got up. He talked about how Harlin hadn't lost his spirit, even when he was in the hospital. He'd thanked God for the nurses and even got one of them to slip him some gin before he died.

At Grace's table, Jack said that Harlin hadn't had any spirit at all. He was just lying there, stupidly, pissing in a bag, and it was Stewart who thanked God for the nurses, one redhead in particular. In fact, it was Stewart who brought in the gin, "for Harlin," which he drank himself until he asked the redheaded nurse if she would come to his house in that uniform and was forced to leave.

Jack and Rusty got up to go smoke, and Grace stretched her legs across their empty chairs, enjoying a little solitude in the crowded room. She looked at the people around her: Earl in his one fine suit checking out Ada Wilder's ass; Ada standing there with her hand on her hip, letting him. Cyrus trying to look over his neck brace and down Janet Wilder's dress, Anne-Marie saying something to Martin, and Martin looking past her as if he'd already heard it a thousand times. After a while it was as if Harlin were everywhere, in every man in the room. And the more she looked, the more it seemed as if every woman was some version of her, or what she might have been if she'd stayed in this world. She missed Harlin terribly then, as much as she missed herself as a younger, wilder woman, and a sweet melancholy went through her—a mix of grief, longing, and love that felt like homesickness.

Yet it was getting later, and the party was starting to turn. Anne-Marie and Martin began to brawl. Someone had written the word "penis" on Anne-Marie's sonogram and drawn an arrow toward what looked like the baby's head. Rusty and Jack came back to the table reeking of pot, complaining about the no smoking laws, and then Jack asked Grace if she wanted to see his tattoos. She said, Sure, why not? and he pulled up his shirt. Inside an uneven circle, a crucifix, halfway filled in, took up most of his chest. "I was going to get one of those Chinese ying-yangs on my stomach," he said, "but I figured that when I got old and all fat, it would stretch out and look weird."

Rusty asked her if she wanted to see his tattoos, too, and pulled up his pant leg to show off what looked like chain mail across his kneecap. Then he showed her more of the same design on his calf. Each tattoo looked homemade, as if Rusty had stabbed himself ten thousand times with a Bic pen. "I got the idea from that game Doom," he said.

Grace smiled weakly.

"Yeah," said Jack. "All he does is sit around and draw medieval shit." He absentmindedly scratched at a scab on his arm. "Show her the best one."

Rusty unbuttoned his shirt and revealed his finest tattoo. It was more chain mail, this time taking up half his chest. When Grace saw it, she gasped, not because the tattoo was startling, which it was, but because through its center, down the middle of Rusty's torso, ran a vertical raised scar, long and thick as a kitchen knife.

The scar was so angry, stuck in the middle of that unfinished ink-blue net, it hurt just to look at it. "Oh, Rusty," Grace said. "What happened to you?"

Rusty looked down at his chest, as if trying to figure out whether she was talking about the scar or the tattoo. "Someone beat me up when I was a baby," he said.

"Here we go," Jack said. "Yeah, yeah, someone dropped you off all messed up at St. Anthony's."

"I had so many broken bones they had to cut me

open," Rusty went on. "The orderly had to hold my heart in his hand and pump it himself to keep me alive."

Grace's head was beginning to swim. It was as if all of these sadnesses—her mother's empty house, Harlin's death, and now this horrible fact—were building on one another, and the weight of them bore down on her heart, opening spaces she thought she'd closed long ago.

"St. Anthony's isn't a hospital, it's a mental institution," she said, although she guessed that both Jack and Rusty knew this already. She knew the place well; she'd driven a food truck there before she'd gotten her job driving for the state prisons. It was a lonesome, rambling brick building with hard lighting and sprawling grounds that had once housed apple orchards and rich gardens. During her first week there, one of the inmates had broken a security guard's legs. This fucking town, she thought. Who would think a loony bin would be a good place for a baby? And who would beat a baby like that? Her own father had waited until she was at least ten before he started in on her, not that that made that jackass any kind of a saint. But a baby. An *infant*. There should be a limit on what people could do.

She reached out and put a hand on Rusty's cheek.

"I'm not real proud of my tattoos," he said. "I was only sixteen when I got most of them."

Cyrus, the last living male Wilder, came over to their table and said he was going to be out drinking that night until he ran out of money. "Then," he said, "I am going to find some more money so I can put it on the Super Bowl."

Jack thought that sounded like a good idea and left without saying goodbye. Grace decided it was time to go, too. She gathered up her purse and sweater, and said goodbye to Rusty, who was still sitting at the table, doodling on a foam cup. She was about to leave when, without looking up from his drawing, Rusty said, "Harlin was the guy who brought me to the mental hospital that night."

Grace stopped.

"I don't know much about it," Rusty said, looking at her now. "He was living downstairs from us then, and I guess my birth mother showed up at his door one night and asked him to get me out of the house."

Grace sat down. She saw the whole thing then: a

frantic woman showing up at Harlin's door; Harlin, annoyed and saddened by the things he had to deal with, agreeing to take her battered child to the hospital. She saw him carefully wrapping Rusty in one of the ratty blankets he kept in the back of his truck and speeding to the hospital without a car seat, accumulating infractions all the way. She imagined that baby, lying in the front seat or across Harlin's lap, unable to cry without breaking something else, and her ex-husband trying to soothe him by singing some old country song about loneliness or bad women. She saw the two of them hurtling through a moonless night and then she saw Harlin pass the hospital, because he was probably drunk and had a police record and wouldn't want to answer any questions, and drive to St. Anthony's, where he probably knew or had had sex with someone who worked there. It was so typical of that man, she thought, to do the right thing and rescue a child but then to end up missing the hospital and drop the baby off at an insane asylum. She imagined him standing there while the orderly took over, unsure of what to do next. Cyrus was right, she thought. There was a lot you could say about Harlin.

"It's funny," Rusty said. "He saved me at the beginning of my life, and then just showed up again near the end of his. Kind of makes you wonder about things."

"I guess," Grace said. She smiled a little sadly. Then she started to laugh. "Harlin," she said. "Jesus Christ. You're lucky he didn't drop you off at a bowling alley."

Rusty laughed, too, and then asked her if she wanted to come out for a drink, but Grace couldn't see her night getting any better if she did.

"Maybe another time," she said.

"You're not bad looking for an older lady," Rusty said. "If things don't work out with your old man, you should call me up."

Outside, Grace stood listening to the night sounds of the place she used to live. It was an early fall night, the kind Harlin had always loved, when there was a bite to the air that stirred things up—people, livestock, the wind and the leaves. Overhead, a flock of geese flew by a half-moon, their wings beating like a wild heart. Grace thought about Rusty starting his life with his heart in someone else's hand, and all the hope he had for his soon-to-be-over marriage and his unborn child. It was the thing that had always gotten her about Harlin, his relentless hope. It was what kept him from being a bad man, and part of what made him a stupid one. She thought about the ex-wife who'd been suing him and wondered if she loved and hated him still.

In the lobby of the hotel, Grace bought a pack of cigarettes and then went back to her room. She was still thinking about Harlin as she took off her panty hose, slipped her underwear off under her skirt, and put on some lipstick. Then she picked up the phone and called Lanford Guthrie, who she knew was at home, waiting, if not for her then for something or someone. "Lanford," she said when he answered the phone. "It's me."

"Grace," he said. "How are you holding up?"

"Good," she said. "Fine. Drunk."

"Should I come over?" he said.

"Yes," Grace said. "I think that would be best."

She turned off the lights in the room and lit a cigarette, and as she sat waiting for Lanford, she drank one more bourbon in Harlin's honor. She thought about how he'd taught her to ride a horse, and to talk dirty, and how long it had been since she'd had sloppy, drunken sex like the kind she was about to have. She thanked Harlin for all that, as she sat there smoking, a habit she'd given up long ago but still loved. He was her best husband, and she was his best wife, and she wanted to do right by him.

Across the street she could see the mourners staggering out of the lodge, two or three at a time, some singing, one woman weeping. "Say what you will about drunks," she said out loud to the dark room around her, "but no one will love you like they can."

ABOUT THE AUTHOR

Rebecca Barry lives in Trumansburg, New York, with her husband and two sons. Her nonfiction has appeared in numerous publications, including *The New York Times Magazine*, *The Washington Post Magazine*, *Seventeen*, *Real Simple*, *Details*, *Hallmark*, and *The Best American Travel Writing 2003*. Her fiction has appeared in *Ploughshares*, *One Story*, *Tin House*, *Ecotone*, *The Mid-American Review*, and *Best New American Voices 2005*.